HOOLIE and the HOOLIGANS
The Alien that ate my Socks

HOOLIE and the HOOLIGANS
The Alien that ate my Socks

written and illustrated by

Brandon Dorman

SHADOW
MOUNTAIN

Visit us at ShadowMountain.com

Library of Congress Cataloging-in-Publication Data

Names: Dorman, Brandon, author, illustrator. | Dorman, Brandon. Hoolie and the hooligans ; book 1.
Title: The alien that ate my socks / written and illustrated by Brandon Dorman.
Description: Salt Lake City, Utah : Shadow Mountain, [2016] | ©2016. | Series: Hoolie and the hooligans ; book 1 | Summary: Henry and his brothers Hank and Hector are simply trying to get in all the fun they can before school starts, when a purple alien monster shows up and messes up their plans.
Identifiers: LCCN 2016005998 | ISBN 9781629722221 (hardbound : alk. paper)
Subjects: LCSH: Brothers—Fiction. | Aliens—Fiction. | CYAC: Brothers—Fiction. | Family life—Fiction. | Extraterrestrial beings—Fiction. | Adventure and adventurers—Fiction. | LCGFT: Action and adventure fiction.
Classification: LCC PZ7.D727596 Al 2016 | DDC [Fic]—dc23
LC record available at http://lccn.loc.gov/2016005998 (CIP data on file)

Printed in the United States of America   06/2016
Lake Book Manufacturing Inc., Melrose Park, IL

10   9   8   7   6   5   4   3   2   1

For my beautiful and golden wife, Emily

Contents

1. The Hooligan Hasher 1

2. The Double Whammy 15

3. What Was That Thing? 28

4. Purple People Eater 38

5. Un-Golden 48

6. What's Up, Doc? 57

7. Thunder and Lightning 72

8. Smoke and Fire 78

9. Smokey the Bear 92

10. What Stinks? 108

11. One Surprising Stomach 127

12. Kapow! Kapow! 134

13. A Field of Stars 141

14. Real Live Alien 152

15. Abduction 165

16. Dr. Brainstrong 179

17. Hoolie Speaks 200

Epilogue 213

CHAPTER 1

The Hooligan Hasher

Hi, I'm Henry. I've had fake front teeth for two years now. I was standing behind my oldest brother, Hank, when we were playing baseball in the street and WHAMMO! Bat to the face.

Man-o-man, it hurt. Hank felt real bad, but the good news is my dad's a dentist. He gave me new teeth and they feel just like the real thing: slimy and hard. That's why I'm not afraid of riding in the front of our go-cart for tomorrow's race. I figure if something gets broken, I'll just get a fake one to replace it.

We worked all summer on our racing machine. We call it the Hooligan Hasher. First because we hope to hash up our competition, and second because we love hash browns for breakfast.

It holds all three of us brothers and it's made from a large piece of irrigation pipe we found in a ditch. We wrapped a metal sheet into a cone and attached it to the front. It's pretty much a missile on wheels! We made it similar to a go-cart in Hank's Boy Scout book with some of our own modifications. It has a spoiler, a side-view mirror, and a windshield—with an electric wiper. Levers run along the inside to where my oldest brother, Hank, sits in the back so he can steer. Since I am the youngest and the smallest I ride in the front, leaving Hector in the middle. Everyone knows that in a race you want the most weight near your back wheels. Hank was a three-time Pinewood Derby champion with this method, so he knows what he's doing. Our plan has Hector and Hank pushing off and jumping in behind me, like a bobsled team.

Since tomorrow is the big race, we looked it over one more time. Hank was standing with his tongue out and eyebrows down, his eyes inspecting everything carefully. Then his tongue slipped back inside his mouth and said, "We need more weight. And since the weight needs to be in the back, we need to shift everything forward."

I reminded him that my legs went in the front and if he was going to shift things forward he was going to have to figure out how to get rid of my legs.

"My legs don't detach, Hank," I pointed out, but then I wondered if fake legs would be better than real ones. Gigi, our grandma, had surgery on her legs and she told us that the doctor gave her bionic knees. She doesn't use a walker anymore. I've asked her at least a hundred times to leap over a house in a single bound. She reassures me she will, if ever an urgent need arises, but it's bad manners to be a showoff. Then there's the man who runs the Gas N' Go, who has a fake eye. I wonder if it's bionic, because it seems like he sees everything that goes on in Skunkerton. That's the name of our town.

We could use some bionic-ness tomorrow.

"The only way Rock can beat us," Hank said, "is with weight. No way whatever he's built is more aerodynamic or has wheels that spin smoother. The heavier we are, the faster we'll fly down Deadman's Hill. So if you must keep your legs, then we'll each have to drink a gallon of water just before the race. By my calculations, that would add at least an extra twenty-five pounds."

"I think Henry should drink a gallon of blended monkey brains," Hector teased. I told him he would look better with monkey lips.

"Better yet," Hank said, ignoring us both, "if we're going to drink a gallon of something, we might as well make it something good. How about orange juice?"

All of us Hooligans love orange juice, especially to dip our toast in.

"It's settled," Hank said. "Twenty-five pounds of orange juice. Other than the weight, all we need to do is paint 'er up and we're golden. We're gonna smoke the old-lady-kisser tomorrow!"

"We gotta paint flames on it!" I said.

Hector laughed. "I think Henry's head would look good with flames on it—real flames." He laughed some more.

I told him if I had some, I would use my head-flames to roast him like a Thanksgiving turkey.

"Flames are cool," Hank said. So we agreed on painting red flames on the side of the Hooligan Hasher. Then we attached a sign on the back that reads ROCK EATS BLENDED MONKEY BRAINS.

Mom and Dad don't know we've built the Hooligan Hasher. This race is just between us three Hooligan brothers and Rock Rubinstein, a big, round-faced bully. He has a twenty-year-old brother who races real race cars, supposedly in the Indian 500. Honestly, I had never heard of a race with five hundred Indians, but it's a big deal, I guess. The only other people who know about our top-secret race are Ellie Einstein and Gwen Gardner. Ellie is going to shoot the gun at the starting line (don't worry though, it's an old cap gun from the dollar store) and Gwen is going to be at the bottom with a checkered tablecloth (also a bargain at the dollar store). We Hooligans love the dollar store. Especially the snack packs—who cares if the expiration date was a year ago? Everything's just a little chewier than normal.

We challenged Rock to the race to settle our ongoing war. It all started last year. Even though we've lived in Skunkerton ever since we can remember, last year was our first year at Fighting Skunk Elementary. It's a brand-new school. About a week after school started, some crazy stuff started happening. One Tuesday our lunch lady, Mrs. Krunk, was sporting a blue upper lip when she served us the mashed potatoes. Apparently somebody had put blue food coloring in her hot chocolate. Then our librarian, Mrs. Booker, jumped out of her socks during third-grade reading time when she opened the book return and two garden snakes slithered out. One went right up her skirt! Two days later, Hank, Hector, and I were walking out of Reading Club and we saw a bucket of

water balancing on the top of the art room door.

"Someone's gonna get cooled off," I said to Hector. "Should we try and get it down?"

"I think we should mind our own beeswax," he said.

"I don't know," Hank said. "You know that Mom would want us to do the right thing. And when we tell Dad how we saved the day, well, he might let us have an extra piece of pie after dinner." Hector loves pie.

"Okay, okay. But if a bunch of bees come swarming out of that bucket I'm outta here," Hector complained.

We pulled a chair over and Hank was trying to take the bucket down, when Principal Pizazz came pizazzing around the corner. Pizazzing is the way he walks—he takes long strides,

swinging his left arm vigorously while keeping his right hand in his pocket. However, this time his right hand came out of his pocket and, using both hands, he grabbed Hector and me by the shirt.

"Caught red-handed!" his voice boomed. "Why am I not surprised? The three Hooligan brothers!"

Let's just say the three of us got blamed for all the chaos that had gone on since the first day of school. We spent two weeks in a new club: The Detention Club. Hector was right. We should have just minded our own beeswax.

Two days later, Rock Rubinstein stuck his foot out and tripped Hank in the hallway. Hank totally biffed it and the chocolate snack pack in his lunch bag squished out all over his shirt. It looked just like the word we're not ever supposed to say at the dinner table. Rock smiled at Hector and me. "That's a warning. Don't mess with my pranks again, or else."

So Rock was the one who'd set up the water bucket above the doorway! I pretended that lasers shot out of my eyes and melted his face into fried dog puke.

The next three days, Hank's lunch went missing from his locker. The only thing left behind was a chocolate snack pack. Something had to be done! Nobody messes with the Hooligan brothers like that, especially if it's a big bully named after dirt.

So we put a squirt gun filled with pink permanent dye inside Rock's locker and rigged up a string that would pull the trigger when the door opened. Ding! Ding! Rock was the winner! Hank said he came to class with a bright pink forehead. Everyone laughed at him. So he broke the handlebars off my scooter. So Hector and I locked him in the bathroom. So he broke Hector's science project into thirty-four pieces. So when Rock fell asleep in class Hank tied his shoelaces together. So he broke all the pencils in Hank's desk and ripped up his homework. So we secretly stuck a sign to his backpack that read, "I love to kiss old-lady lips."

Finally, after no sign of either side backing down and three trips to the principal's office, Hank proposed a race to settle our feud. A secret race. Over the summer we would build homemade go-carts and race down Deadman's Hill the week before school started again. If we won, Rock would kiss Mrs. Krunk, the lunch lady, and quit all pranks for the entire year. If Rock won, we agreed to do one prank a week for him for the whole year—on whoever he'd choose. Sounds extreme, I know, but those are the only terms Rock would agree to. The witness was Ellie Einstein, a girl in Hank and Rock's class. I still tell

Hank we should have never agreed. I would like to spray paint Rock's bike pink with sparkles, add a flower basket and bow on the front, and sign him up for the town parade. And no matter the outcome of the race, I still might sign him up for a subscription to *UWWM—Ultra Women's Wrestling Magazine*.

"You know you're going to lose, right?" Rock said every time we saw him. "My brother is a professional racer and he taught me how to win. And when I win, your first prank will be to color Mr. Walters's glasses black with a permanent marker. Then he won't see me break your ears in band class, Hank."

Broken ears don't scare me. I'd just get bionic ones. But Hector disagreed. "No breaking any bones, Rock, or the deal's off!"

"There are no bones in your ears," Rock snarled with a smile. "It's cartilage. Oh, and since there are three of you, I'll have Bugs and Bunny onboard with me during the race. See you the final week of the summer at the top of Deadman's Hill."

"Who are Bugs and Bunny?" I asked after Rock was gone.

"Probably the stuffed animals he cuddles with at night," Hank said.

"If we lose," Hector said, "I'm moving to Hawaii."

"Hawaii?" I asked, my eyebrows up.

"So I can make friends with buff Polynesians who'll protect me," he said. "And I think coconuts would make good weapons to defend myself, although they would probably just ricochet off Rock's thick head."

That had been almost eight weeks ago.

We finished our inspection of the Hooligan Hasher and Hank asked Hector and me to put one last coat of Crisco on the axles. That makes the wheels spin freely for almost three minutes straight.

"With the added weight, we won't have a problem with speed," Hank said. Deadman's Hill is steep. It's on the edge of town and more of a mountain than a hill. A while ago we hiked around it and it took us almost ten hours. A single-lane road runs from top to bottom, but cars no longer drive up it because of a roadblock that was put in place years ago. And the road goes nowhere except to the top of the hill. The road isn't straight, though. It winds back and forth and there are three blind corners where you can't see what's around the bend. But I'm not afraid. We've taken the Hasher for two test runs and know just how to take each blind turn. I have no clue if Rock has done the same over the summer, but if not, he'll probably fly off the edge and break one of his own bones. We don't even know why it's called Deadman's Hill. We've found eleven dead skunks on the hill, but no dead men. Yet.

After the final coat of Crisco, Hank called us over to a

miniature model of the hill he'd made out of random tools from the shed. Hank had made Hector and me memorize every turn.

"Remember," he said, "the most important part, other than the start, is slowing with the hand brake just before the double whammy on turn six. That's all you, Henry."

I nodded.

"After that, we tuck and let gravity pull us to victory. We totally got this, guys."

"You sure we'll win?" Hector asked.

"Pretty sure." Hank must have thought Hector needed some reassurance. "Look, if we lose, I'll let you dump fifty grasshoppers down the back of my pants." Hank laughed.

Hector grinned but then looked flustered. "Wait—you just said that because you know I'll never find fifty grasshoppers."

"Deadman's Hill is full of grasshoppers!" I reminded him.

Hector grinned at me.

Hank glared at me.

I just shrugged and smiled.

We put the paint away and for the first time we didn't cover the racing machine. Hopefully, the newly painted red flames would dry by morning.

CHAPTER 2

The Double Whammy

At breakfast, Mom asked us what we had planned for the day. "Only five more days of summer left," she said with a smile. "Would you like to go to the swim park?"

"Henry would," volunteered Hector. "But you better bring his swim diaper."

I reminded Hector he swims like a horse, with his tongue out and eyes bulging.

Hank rolled his eyes and told her we were busy with a super-dangerous race that was going to affect the outcome of our entire school year.

"Super-dangerous race, huh?" she repeated. "You know you have your chores to do before any playing takes place."

"Easy peasy lemon squeezy," Hank replied. And we all promised to have everything done before an ounce of racing took place.

Mom had her gardening club at ten that morning so we got right to it and raced through our chores. I took out the garbage, Henry cleaned up the garage, and Hank mowed the lawn—all by the time Mom pulled out of the driveway. We headed back to the old shed and opened the doors. The bright red Hooligan Hasher sat waiting for us, flames and all. Three gallons of orange juice waited for us, too.

"Where did you get that?" I asked.

"Never mind that—let's get drinking," Hank replied.

"*What?* You were serious?" Hector exclaimed.

"Look, isn't a little bladder discomfort worth it for a whole year free from the old-lady-kisser?" Hank asked. "And it's powdered orange juice from the food storage. I mixed it up last night."

I could tell Hector wasn't convinced, but he picked up his gallon. It took us about thirty minutes to each drink our gallon. I felt sick. I gagged once and sprayed orange juice out my nose. It stung, but Hank cheered us on and promised the extra weight would give us the edge. I gulped the rest of it down.

The paint on our racing machine was dry and it looked amazing in the sun as we loaded it onto the old Radio Flyer wagon pulled by Hank's bike. Hank hollered at me to grab the helmets.

The top of Deadman's Hill was about twelve blocks away, on the edge of town. We took back roads to avoid as many eyes as possible. But when we passed the Gas N' Go, I'm sure the man with the glass eye saw us—you can't avoid a bionic eye.

Ellie Einstein was waiting when we arrived and she let us know that Gwen was waiting at the bottom. Ellie had already marked a starting line with chalk and she gave the cap gun a test shot. There was no sign of Rock yet. Ellie talked mainly to Hank since they're in the same class.

"So, are you ready to smoke the socks off Rock?" she asked. "I hope you do, because his socks really do stink. I have to sit in front of him in Cultures class and my eyes water the whole period. I'm hoping you toast those puppies just so I can see the chalkboard again. "

The sun was out, so Hank slipped his sunglasses on and tried to act cool.

He told Ellie she didn't need to worry because toasting Rock's socks was his specialty. Then we heard the sound of barking dogs. From behind us came two big black Rottweilers pulling a sleek

black mace-like thing on six wheels. It looked like a bad replica of the Batmobile. Rock Rubinstein was inside holding a rope that was attached to each spiked collar, like he was driving a sleigh with two horses. Ugly horses.

"Whoa there, Bugs. Whoa there, Bunny," Rock called out.

"He's racing with those walruses?" Hector said to me under his breath. "We have a better chance of making the high school cheer squad than outweighing those things."

"I bet you'd look look good on the cheer squad with your pom-poms," I snickered.

"Oh, yeah? Well, your . . . head is a pom-pom," Hector said.

I thought that was a pretty lame comeback but I didn't say it because it was obvious that Hector was nervous about Bugs and Bunny.

Rock got out of his black rocket and walked closer to us. "Hey there, Ellie. Glad you agreed to watch me scorch these dweebs in a race. Most likely I'll get to the bottom before you can blink your pretty little eyelashes. You know, my older brother . . ."

" . . . races Formula One cars?" she finished his sentence.

"Yeah, pretty much the coolest racer ever in the whole world. So I'm going to burn these three hooli-babies like charred hot dogs and enjoy a whole year of breaking everything Hooligan," Rock finished.

I felt my eye lasers heating up. "The only thing that's gonna be broken this year, you meathead, is your mouth when Mrs.

Krunk kisses you so hard it falls off," I taunted. "And all we'll see are those two big ol' buck teeth of yours and we'll rename you Beaver."

Rock glared at me. "Hank, your brother's voice is so high it sounds like a chihuahua. Bugs and Bunny eat chihuahuas for lunch."

"Let's settle this on the road," Hank said.

"Bring it."

Hector and I pulled our racing machine up to Ellie's starting line. As I climbed into my spot I heard the orange juice slosh around in my stomach. I felt a little sick. Hector put a hand on his stomach, too.

Rock lined up his black rocket and whistled to his two pet monsters. They scrambled inside, slobbering and foaming at the mouth. Something told me they had practiced for this.

"Helmets on," Ellie called out.

Rock's helmet was decorated with spikes and his face oozed out the bottom.

"Get ready," Ellie yelled and raised the cap gun.

Hank and Hector started

rocking the Hooligan Hasher back and forth like they do at the beginning of a bobsled race. I put my feet up inside the nosecone. Rock took his stance and glared over at me. He mouthed the word "chihuahua" and blew me a kiss.

"3 . . . 2 . . . 1 . . ." Bang! Ellie pulled the trigger.

I felt the jolt from behind and a little bit of orange juice sloshed up the back of my throat. Both cars shot past the starting line fast, but Hank and Hector managed to push ahead of the black rocket a little and with an extra shove they jumped in behind me.

The launch was good, probably our best yet. About twenty-five yards off the starting line the hill dipped and we picked up speed. I glanced in the rearview mirror and saw two big pink tongues flapping right on our tail. My heart was thumping super-fast. Turn one came sooner than I remembered. But when Hank yelled, "*LEAN!*" I leaned and felt Hector do the same. One down, five to go.

"*LEAN!*" Hank yelled again.

We leaned three more times. Right. Left. Right. With each turn, I began to feel more and more sick. We managed to pull ahead of Rock by about five feet, but I could still see dog teeth, fangs more like, in my mirror. Let's just say the objects were closer than they appeared.

On turn four it happened.

We took the corner faster than expected—it must have been the extra Crisco on the axles because the Hooligan Hasher tipped up on its two left wheels. When the right wheels hit the pavement again, most of the gallon of orange juice in my small body spewed from my mouth and shot out my nose.

Hector and Hank yelled behind me, "Ahhhkkk!"

We swayed as they struggled to wipe the vomit out of their eyes and off their faces, but we kept going.

"Sorry!" I apologized. But really, I felt a whole lot better.

I heard Hector say "Yuck! I got some in my mou—"

But before he could finish, his insides exploded, too. Most of his orange juice shot over the side.

We'd lost speed and out of the corner of my eye I saw two big black heads pull alongside us. The barf juice must have missed

Rock and the monsters. Or maybe they just slurped it right up. They probably love barf juice.

The worst was still ahead though. Turn six: the double whammy, a sharp S-curve. The first turn was blind because of a huge boulder on the left side. But we had practiced and as long as I slowed us down just before the turn, we'd be golden. I heard Hank yelling to remind me to pull on the brake. I knew I could do it. No sweat.

But just before I yanked up on the wooden lever, my mouth dropped open. My eyes must have looked like two Frisbees when an enormous, um, *thing* popped up from behind the boulder! It landed on two legs right smack-dab in the middle of the road.

"Aaaaggghhh!" Hector shouted.

All I could see was a huge purple blur as Hank swerved us hard to the right. The Hooligan Hasher left the road and took flight over the side of the hill.

Now, I have "gotten air" on my bike before, even enough to

brag about, but at this moment we were so high we could have easily made the cover of *Super Mad Air* magazine.

Everything moved in slow motion until *SMASH* we landed back on the earth and connected hard with the rocks and overgrown grass. We bounced twice before straightening out and shooting down the hill. The Hooligan Hasher had turned into a full-blown off-road racing machine.

"Hang on!" yelled Hank.

"You think so?" Hector yelled back. "I'm really tempted to just let go. Psych!"

Hank tried to steer, but the side of the hill was much steeper than the road, and any quick turns would no doubt fling our three elementary-school bodies off into oblivion.

"*PULL THE BRAKE!*" Hank commanded.

Oh yeah, I thought. *Duh*. But when I pulled up on the wooden hand brake, it broke right off!

"Umm, guys . . ." I started. "The brake is no longer an option!"

"*WHAT?*" Hector cried. "What should we do?"

"*JUST HANG ON!*" Hank yelled.

Truthfully, that was all we could do as we barreled down the rest of Deadman's Hill, through the boulders, grass, dirt, brush, and hundreds of grasshoppers jumping for their lives.

We hit the bottom of the hill like a runaway freight train. We smashed through the Flannigans' wooden fence and through their flowerbeds, taking out four lawn gnomes and a birdbath as we passed.

As luck would have it, Mrs. Flannigan was down on her hands and knees weeding so we didn't hit her. But she did let loose with a shrill scream and flung her trowel into the air.

We had so much momentum, the Hooligan Hasher shot through the yard and barreled across the street. We jumped the curb and took out the Campbells' mailbox and trash cans. We finally came to a crashing halt when we hit old Mr. Hudson's front door. When I heard his doorbell ring I looked up and

saw a large stick poking out of my helmet. It must have rung the bell just as we stopped. What are the chances of that? One in a million? A billion? Cool!

Well, I thought, *at least we're not dead.*

The three of us climbed out of the car. Covered in dirt and dead grass, we looked like commandos decked out in natural camouflage. The Hooligan Hasher was dented, scratched, and if it had had an engine, it would definitely have been billowing smoke.

The front door opened and we looked up to see Mr. Hudson glaring down at us. A year ago, Mr. Hudson had caught us toilet-papering his porch and we'd spent the better part of a day cleaning it up. The funny thing was we hadn't actually done it. The kids who had done it had taken off long before we showed up. When my mom saw the bathroom tissue as she was driving home she asked her three sons to do the right thing and clean up the mess. And we were trying to clean it up when Mr. Hudson came out and accused us of doing the deed. So to begin with we really didn't have a great relationship with Mr. Hudson.

"I hope we won," Hector groaned.

But then I noticed the grasshoppers jumping out of Hank's pants.

CHAPTER 3

What Was That Thing?

To say we were in trouble was an understatement. Mom was a patient person, but she got really flustered if she missed her gardening club meetings. And to be interrupted right in the middle to come pick up her three boys because they had just destroyed a fence, a flowerbed, four lawn gnomes, a mailbox, and a door got her blood boiling.

"You should have seen the look Betty Black gave me," she told us, her eyes dashing up to the rearview mirror to look at us. "I'm sure all the women there were thinking the same thing: *Those boys are always messing up something; no wonder their name is Hooligan.*"

Hank, Hector, and I sat in the back seat, elbow to elbow, still covered in dirt and twigs. We all knew we had a great mom; she was just blowing off steam.

Hector was super-grumpy, too. Hank looked frustrated. I was itchy. I think there was some grass in my pants.

"What happened just before the double whammy?" I whispered to Hank.

"Your girly hands didn't pull the brake and slow us down," Hector interrupted.

"I was about to," I said. "But then there was that big ol' *thing* that jumped out in front of us—what in the world *was* that?"

"I don't know," Hank said. "It all happened so fast I didn't get a good look at it. I just tried to miss it."

"You missed it alright," Hector said. "And now we've lost the race and Rock is going to break my ears! Seriously, I'm moving to Hawaii."

"Maybe not," I said. "Rock was right behind us, so he either smashed into the purple blob or went off the road as well."

The car pulled into our driveway and Mom made us get out and stand on the lawn. She sprayed us down with the hose and informed us we would be doing work around the house until Dad got home that evening. Together, they would decide our fate and punishment.

"Of course, you'll be fixing the Flannigans' fence and re-planting Mrs. Flannigan's flowers. The Campbells' mailbox will need to be replaced, and you'll need to earn the money for Mr. Hudson's new porch door," Mom said.

"Bag of hair!" Hector exclaimed. He used that instead of a curse word. He used to say something else but got Hooligan Hot Sauce for his trouble, so he just started saying *bag of hair* instead. It started after Mom cut our hair once and he dropped the bag of hair clippings on his laundry pile and it got all over his clean underwear. He was itchy for a week.

Mom assigned me to scrub the tile in the bathroom, Hector to wash all the windows, and Hank had to paint the shed.

Later that night at dinner Dad was quiet as Mom explained the day's events.

"So your cart is back in the shed, but I'd really like you to explain why you were riding it down Deadman's Hill," Dad asked. "That's a very dangerous place."

We looked at each other until, finally, Hank spoke up. "We were racing Rock Rubinstein."

"I see," Dad said. "Well, I expect you to be at Mrs. Flannigan's at nine A.M. sharp and then spend all day there tomorrow. I've already talked with her and the Campbells and Mr. Hudson. Your mother and I assured them you'll fix what you've broken. But you also need to come up with a way to earn the money to replace Mr. Hudson's door."

"Yessir," we replied in unison and looked down at our plates.

After dinner the three of us were sent to bed a little early. As we walked back to our shared bedroom, Dad said, "And tonight I want you to come up with a plan so this doesn't happen again."

He says that after all our adventures that go wrong. He said it after we made magical growing potions for Mom's pink lilies out of lemon juice, vinegar, soap, and vitamin tablets. (Those didn't work.) He said it after we rolled down the car windows and tried to wash the inside and the outside at the same time. (That didn't work either.) And he said it with really low eyebrows after we

puppy-sat for Mrs. Deasey. We left all the doors open so her new bulldog, Frauw-Frauw, could enjoy the yard on a sunny day. Well, we got involved in a pretty ferocious game of warball that night . . . and forgot to go back. Mrs. Deasey came home to a house full of skunks and one very stinky puppy.

We were quiet in our beds for a long while. Hector had pulled out one of his *Biology Blasters* magazines and was grumpily reading about prehistoric cats and life on Mars. I was about to fall asleep when Hector spoke up.

"How in the world are we going to earn enough money to buy a door? I mean, who needs doors anyway? Can't we just be a doorless town? Everyone would save a lot of money not having to buy doors. A new door is probably like a hundred billion dollars."

"Try a hundred billion minus the billion," Hank, who obviously wasn't sleeping either, answered. "We can earn a hundred dollars by doing a car wash or something."

"Or sell hamdogs!" I suggested. Hamdogs are a hamburger-

hotdog mix we Hooligan brothers invented a few summers ago.

"What I just can't figure out is what that thing was that jumped out in front of us," Hank said.

"It was purple," I added.

"The only thing that should be purple are your

fingernails," grunted Hector. "You and your girly hands couldn't pull a simple brake."

I reminded Hector that his favorite toy when he was five was a Barbie.

Then Hank said, "I want to go back up to the double whammy and see if we can find out what it was. Maybe it lives up there in the rocks?"

"No chance we'll get back up there," Hector said. "We'll be working to fix this mess all day every day for like . . . forever."

"Exactly. Dad said we had chores all day tomorrow. He didn't say anything about *tonight*," Hank said.

I had dozed off a little but was startled awake by Hank's idea.

"*What?*" Hector blurted out. "You want us to go *now*? Are you crazy? If Mom and Dad catch us . . ."

I sat up and interrupted Hector. "Dad did tell us to figure out a plan so this doesn't happen again."

"That's right," Hank nodded. "And finding that purple thing is the first part of our plan. Dad should be glad that we're really thinking this through."

I looked at Hank. Coolest. Brother. Ever.

Hector shook his head in disbelief. "If we get caught, Dad will add stuff to our list of chores, like putting in a sprinkler system and rotating the tires on the car. Maybe even re-roofing the house. You know he will."

"Look, we'll leave a note in our room explaining that we

took Dad's advice and that we'll be back soon," Hank explained. "I doubt they'll even know we're gone."

It sounded good to me. "I'm in!" I said.

Hank put on some dark clothes and I followed his lead. With a big scowl on his face, Hector did the same. I reached under my mattress, grabbed three large granola bars, and put them in my back pockets. Sometimes I get hungry in the middle of the night so it's much easier to have a midnight stash instead of rummaging through the kitchen in the dark.

As Hank wrote the note, Hector said, "Maybe you should write that Henry had a nightmare that he ran out of purple fingernail polish, so he crawled out the window, and we had to chase him down."

"Ha-ha," I said. "I think you should write that Hector wet himself so we crawled out the window to buy him some more diapers."

Hank ignored both of us. Like follow-the-leader, we tiptoed across the room and slithered out our bedroom window like ninjas. Living in a small rambler definitely had its advantages.

Since our bikes were in the back of Dad's truck, we had to unload them quietly. We took off down the street, taking a shortcut through the Gavins' backyard. We tried to avoid most of the street lamps but did have to pass by the Gas N' Go. I glanced over, and sure enough, the man with the glass eye was there, and looking right in our direction. Creepy.

When we arrived at Deadman's Hill we started hiking near

the tracks we had made earlier. According to my football watch, it took us nine minutes and thirty-two seconds to get to the double whammy. When we were about twenty feet from the road, Hank stuck a finger in front of his mouth and motioned for us to proceed slowly. Hector seemed really uneasy. I was nervous, too.

We came to the road and saw skid marks marking the spot where we flew off the side of the hill.

"Keep your eyes peeled," Hank said.

"I'd rather be peeling a potato at home," Hector grumbled.

I told Hector his brain resembles a potato. He told me to go suck on a potato.

As we climbed over, around, and in between the big rocks near the turn, I suddenly caught a whiff of an unfamiliar aroma. We all wrinkled our noses at the same time.

"Yo—something smells like rotten rat guts and Dad's morning breath blended together," Hector whispered.

I had my nose buried in my shirt when we jumped down into a cluster of rocks and hit the jackpot. Well, if finding an enormous blubbery purple monster with a huge tail and two antennae qualifies as a jackpot.

"Holy bag of hair!" Hector's eyes got wide. Hank's jaw dropped. My nose came out of my shirt.

Then all three of us turned and scrambled right back up the rocks. On the other side we quickly interlocked arms. There's no better way to work through things than in a Hooligan Huddle.

"Okay, we found it. But what in the world is it?" Hector asked.

"No clue," Hank said. "I've never seen anything like it."

"TOLD YOU it WAS PURPLE," I added.

"Let's make like a bakery truck and haul buns home," Hector said.

"Wait!" Hank said. "Let's get one more look. I think it was asleep."

"*NO!*" Hector said. "I'm taking zero chance of becoming dinner to that thing. Maybe there really is a flying purple people eater after all! And the key word is *people eater*!"

"That's two words," I corrected.

Hector scowled and told me to eat a worm. This is what he always says when he wants me to stop talking because, let's face it, it's hard to talk when slurping a worm.

"I'm with you, Hank," I said.

So we broke the huddle, but Hector didn't budge.

Hank and I climbed to the top of the rock again without him, got on our bellies, and peered down. But the purple monster wasn't there. We turned back to look at Hector. And he wasn't there either!

Both the monster and Hector had vanished!

CHAPTER 4

Purple People Eater

My arms grew instant giant goosebumps.

I whispered to Hank, "Where's Hector?"

Hank looked at me, eyebrows down. "This is not good, little bro."

We were about to climb down when we smelled that horrible smell again. Below us, the monster walked into view. He was holding Hector in his arms. My brother's face was buried into what must be the monster's chest. The monster didn't seem to notice me and Hank on top of the rock.

"Should we jump up and scream?" I whispered.

Hank shook his head. "He might run off with Hector, or squeeze him to death or something."

"Yeah, that could get really gross and messy," I said.

Speaking of messy, it looked like little purple pieces of the monstrosity were actually shedding onto the ground. Here and there I could see little blobs of purple mixed with the rocks and grass. But the biggest problem at that moment was how we were going to get Hector out of this hullabaloo.

After a few moments the monster loosened his grip. Hector looked like a wet noodle. He was all limp and didn't make a sound. The monster laid him down on the ground and did the strangest thing. He ran his antennae all over Hector, from head to toe. When the monster got to Hector's feet, he took off Hector's shoes. Then, one after the other, the purple monster ate them.

Hank's eyebrows shot up and his mouth dropped open. Then the monster took off Hector's shorts and ate those too.

Hank turned to me. "Maybe you're right, little bro. Screaming might be appropriate under the circumstances."

We knew we had to intervene. Mom would've intervened had she been there. But it was a good thing she wasn't because, let's face it, we really shouldn't have been there no matter what Hank's note had said.

"We better make it quick," I whispered, "because there go his socks and I'm pretty sure his underwear is next."

Hank counted to three and we leaped off the rock. We screamed and yelled and waved our arms. My eyeballs bounced around in my head and my tongue flapped back and forth like I was the walking dead.

The purple people eater jerked. It jumped to the side and scrambled back ten yards or so. We'd obviously startled it. Hank had his arms up with his hands in zombie position. Both of us snarled like ravenous zombie wolves. I was surprised at how much saliva my little mouth could produce as spit dribbled down my chin. It was kinda gross, but it worked. Either the purple people eater didn't like dripping saliva or we really did look like ravenous zombie wolves. Whatever the case, the super-stinky monster backed behind a large boulder. He must have thought he was being sneaky or something, but I could still see his two antennae poking up over the top.

"I think it's still watching us with its head thingies," I mouthed sideways to Hank.

"I don't care what it's doing as long as it's not eating any more of Hector," Hank replied.

We heard a low, quiet groan from our slimy brother.

I turned slightly and peeked back. Hector's eyelids were closed, but I could tell he was still alive because he was trying to raise his hand to his mouth and say something. It sounded something like "pizza." But it was too mumbled for me to really tell for sure.

Hank and I shuffled back and lifted Hector to a sitting position. He must have been trying to be a ravenous zombie wolf, too, because he was drooling—a lot. I wiped my own mouth first with my sleeve and then Hector's. Gross. Us Hooligan brothers had done a lot together, but I'm pretty sure this was the first time we'd all drooled together.

I glanced up again to check on the monster. The two antennae were still there, bobbing just above the boulder. The bad smell hadn't gone anywhere either.

"We need to make like a banana and split," Hank said. "Before the purple people eater gets brave and realizes we're not zombie wolves."

"You think we can carry Hector?" I asked.

"The only option I see is to do the two-man carry," Hank replied. "Have you learned that in Cub Scouts yet?"

"I'm only a Tiger Cub. The only things we've done are make holiday decorations for the nursing home and paper-sack squirrel puppets," I complained.

"Okay, well, you're going to have to prove you're more than a Tiger Cub tonight," Hank said.

He showed me how to stoop and lock our hands and wrists under Hector's legs and then again behind Hector's back.

"Okay, we're in position," Hank said. "Now, on the count of three, we'll slowly stand up."

As the two of us stood up with Hector scrunched in between us, I felt my arms start to burn. Hector's head fell back limply and he tried to say something. It still sounded like "pizza." He was heavy, at least eighty pounds I guessed. I only weighed fifty-seven pounds—after all the drooling, probably fifty-six.

I told Hank I didn't think I could make it all the way home like this. My arms felt like they were going to break.

"Don't worry, little bro," he said. "I have a plan."

It took us twelve minutes and forty-seven seconds to get to the bottom of the hill; longer than going up because my hand slipped twice and we dropped Hector and his elbow hit a rock. I apologized, but I don't know if he understood me. If he had, he probably would have told me to eat a dead rat or something. And I would have told him he looked like roadkill wearing underwear.

"So what's the plan?" I asked Hank.

"Colin Cooper's skateboard," Hank replied.

"What? You're going to ask Colin Cooper to borrow his skateboard?" I glanced at my watch. "It's almost ten o'clock at night!"

"Well, yes and no. We are going to borrow it now and write him an IOU," Hank said. "He leaves it on his back porch at night."

"An IOU?" I said.

"Yeah. If you leave an IOU, it's not stealing," Hank explained.

I didn't really understand but he told me to just trust him and we headed to Colin Cooper's house. Luckily he only lived two doors down from the Flannigans. Yes, the same Flannigans with the broken-fence-mashed-up-flower-bed-and-garden. So we didn't have far to go.

We laid Hector on the ground and Hank told me not to move or get eaten. I watched him scale the Coopers' fence and drop down the other side. I thought my oldest brother was most definitely half ninja and half Jedi master,

because I did not hear a sound. I peeked through the fence slats and saw his dark silhouette move across the lawn. He carefully picked up something long and tucked it under his arm. But before he headed back, I saw him stoop down and write something in a sandbox near the porch. When he finished, he stepped around the other side of the sandbox and made his way back across the yard. The silence was interrupted when my football watch sounded. "Beep-beep, beep-beep!" Ten o'clock!

As if that was the signal, whoosh! The Coopers' sprinklers popped up and took aim at the intruder, Hank Hooligan.

"Bag of hair!" I yelped. Still peering through the fence, I felt my eyebrows shoot way up.

Hank got blasted in the back of the head first and then in the gut. The sprinklers showed no mercy! He got hit four more times before he slipped on the wet grass and collided with the fence. It was loud. (I take the ninja part back, but he probably still had a little Jedi left in him).

The next thing I knew, a sleek longboard came flying over the fence. Its back wheels smacked Hector's knee. Ouch! That had to hurt. But like I said earlier, if something breaks we'll just get a bionic replacement. Golden!

A soaking-wet Hank followed the skateboard over the fence. Mom would have most likely told him he looked like a drowned muskrat, and I would have agreed. Frantically, Hank heaved Hector up and over one shoulder and told me to grab the board. We both moved fast.

"Do they teach that one-man carry in Cub Scouts too?" I asked, watching Hector's limp body bounce up and down on Hank's shoulder.

"Nope, little bro. I saw a fireman do this once. Always wanted to try it," he replied.

We quickly made our way back around the row of houses and on to Main Street. Our bikes were where we'd left them. I dropped the longboard and helped Hank place Hector face-up on top. I took off my jacket, folded it, and placed it under his head. It looked like a stretcher on wheels.

"But how in the world are we going to make sure he stays on?" I asked. "His legs and arms are hanging off."

"Take off your shoelaces," he replied. "And I'll need the belt you're wearing, too."

Hank's laces were nice and stretchy since they were full of water. While we tied Hector to the longboard, I saw his eyes fixed on me beneath his droopy eyelids. I was quite certain he was telling me to go eat rotten rhino snot in his mind (because

that was something he'd say), but I whispered back, "Don't worry, Hector—Hank and I are going to get you home." And then I smiled and added, "And *you* smell like rotten rhino snot." Because he really did.

CHAPTER 5

Un-Golden

With Hector strapped to the mobile stretcher and the stretcher-longboard tied behind Hank's bike, we took off for home.

I rode on Hector's bike with one hand—which was way too big for me by the way—and also held on to my bike's handlebars right beside me. It seemed to work if I went slow. The only thing that didn't work were my pants—without a belt they kept slipping down. After at least a billion times reaching back to pull them up, I gave in and let them hang and rub on the tire. Oh, yeah, and because my laces were gone, both my shoes fell off too. But nothing short of an alien invasion would have made me go back for them.

My football watch read 10:32 when we pulled into our

driveway. The lights in the house were all out. Quickly and quietly, we put our bikes in the back of Dad's truck and hauled Hector around to our bedroom window.

"I can't believe we might actually pull this off without Mom and Dad suspecting a thing," I whispered to Hank.

"We're not clear yet, little bro. If we can get Hector off the board and back in bed, then we'll be golden," Hank replied and gave me a wink—seriously, the super-most-awesomest brother ever.

We untied Hector and stood him up. Though he still smelled absolutely rotten, he actually seemed to be less wet-noodle-ish than before. I took that as a good sign. Hopefully, the monster's poison would wear off by morning. My hopes of this night ending without detection were getting higher and higher. That is, until we smelled something worse than Hector. Something . . . familiar.

"Do you think it's . . . ?" I whispered to Hank.

"Yep," he replied. "There is only one thing that smells that bad, and it's purple."

"Don't tell me it followed us home!" I said.

"Hurry, let's get Hector through the window."

Our window was easily opened from the outside. You just had to push up on the glass. We would be in real trouble if someone tried to burglarize us, but that hadn't happened yet.

After the window was wide open, Hank and I both crouched

down and put one hand under Hector's bum while we each held one of his arms. His head was pointed right at the opening. We hurried and stood up straight. Hector swayed my way a bit and bang! his forehead connected with the windowpane.

"Whoops," Hank mumbled. "Second time's the charm."

"He's going to hate us forever," I said.

To fix the problem, Hank crouched a little and let Hector lean his way a bit. We both heaved. Hector's head and shoulders made it through but his rear end was still pointed out the window. At that moment I wished I had a bionic eye

that could take pictures on demand. A shot of Hector hanging halfway out a window with no pants, wearing only Incredible Hulk underwear, would have been over-the-top priceless. It would have been the best blackmail material ever known to mankind. I bet I could've convinced him to do all of my chores for the rest of my life.

But I didn't have a bionic eye yet, so the image would have to be forever seared in my previously pure memory instead.

"One more push," Hank said.

"Okay! Go!" I said.

We heaved Hector's legs once more and heard Hector slide through and thud onto the floor.

"I hope that was his shoulder that hit first," I said. I also hoped he didn't remember any of this when the sun came up.

"Me too," Hank said. "But let's get ourselves in first and then we'll worry about him. I have a funny feeling Mr. Purple People Eater is close."

I put a foot in Hank's hands and he hoisted me through the window. He hid the longboard, grabbed any incriminating evidence and then jumped up and slid through as well. I shut the window and crumpled on my bed. Hector's monster-hug stench filled the room.

"Should we try to give him a bath?" I asked Hank.

"Good idea, but no," he said. "That would just be weird. Let's wrap him in blankets and put him in bed. It'll contain the smell."

"Roger that." I had just started wrapping Hector up like a mummy when our bedroom light flipped on. Both Hank and I turned and squinted into the brightness.

Standing in the doorway were our parents. Through squinty eyes I could see they both had upside-down smiles. Hank and I loosened our grip on Hector and the blankets fell off.

"What in Holy Hepsibah's name is going on in here?" Mom said. "And where is that absolutely awful rotten smell coming from?"

We could tell Dad smelled it, too, because his nose was scrunched up like he'd run into a wall.

"And why do you look like a drowned muskrat, Hank?" Mom continued. "And Henry, why are you dressed like a ninja? And Hector, what in Peaceable Percy's name are you doing without any pants?! And what are you two doing with your brother all wrapped up like a mummy?"

These were all reasonable questions. The problem was, we really had no idea how to explain any one of them, let alone all six. So we just kind of stood there.

"Well?" Mom asked, again.

"Umm . . . well . . . err . . . ," Hank began. But before another "well" could stumble out of his mouth, a noise from the roof made his eyebrows shoot up and we all raised our chins to the ceiling. We weren't expecting Rudolph for another four months and it was definitely not the Tooth Fairy. So either the Easter

Bunny was confused about the date or the one thing we feared most had found us.

I looked at Hank.

"THIS CAN'T GET MORE UN-GOLDEN, CAN IT?" I asked. I felt my eyebrows crunch into the "very worried" position.

Before Hank could utter a word, the roof creaked again. And in one giant avalanche, the ceiling gave way and an enormously large purple creature with two bobbing antenna and a tail crashed to the floor.

The sound was deafening. Dust and dirt plumed all around us. Mom started to cough and Dad reached around to shield her from the debris. Hank and I dropped Hector, who crumpled to the floor, and we could only manage four words: "Holy Bag of Hair!"

Shingles and wood peppered the ground and our bedroom light swung free of the ceiling. A portion of the outside wall fell in and for a few seconds I just kept my eyes closed.

Mom always said there were no monsters under my bed. She was right. The monster was on *top* of my bed. Actually, he'd crushed it!

When everything started to settle we could hear Mom and Dad calling to see if we were still in one piece. Well, I guess technically three pieces. Their complete frustration and anger had turned into utter concern. That was a sign that we have really

good parents. Though that could soon change once they realized we were just fine.

"Maybe we should fake being hurt so they'll go easy on us," I coughed to Hank.

"Tempting, little bro," he coughed back. "But if they found out we were faking, we'd be in for Hooligan Hot Sauce!" Both of us shuddered. Hooligan Hot Sauce was the consequence for breaking the number-one rule: Never lie. It was a very unique blend that Mom had made up, and it was especially toxic for liars. The first time I'd had it, I actually felt real steam burst out of my ears.

"Yes, ma'am, we're alright!" we both called out together.

"I didn't hear Hector," I heard Dad say.

In my opinion that was also a sign of a good parent. They could distinguish which voice belongs to which child even in the chaos of a recently caved-in bedroom.

Hector managed to respond. "PiZZA! PiZZA!" he mumbled.

"Hey that was pretty good!" I told him. "You're not secretly the guy on the Little Caesar's commercials, are you?"

He managed to stick his tongue out at me. I smiled and returned the gesture and knew he was going to be just fine. Though the bump on his forehead was really black and blue now.

Once they'd made sure we were okay, my parents switched their focus to the elephant in the room—the purple, trunkless elephant that was currently eating all our bedding and clothes.

CHAPTER 6

What's Up, Doc?

What in Holy Hepsibah's name is that thing, Herman?" we heard Mom ask.

She and Dad stood looking at the monster. Though on closer observation it didn't really seem like a monster. Monsters usually wanted to rip your face off with their fangs. This big fella neither had fangs nor seemed interested in anything but T-shirts and tighty whities, which he seemed to be eating with joy. Personally, he could have all of those he wanted. Most of mine were hand-me-downs anyway. Maybe now Mom would get me some cool Batman underwear.

"I have no idea what that is, dear," I heard Dad reply. He disappeared for a moment then quickly reappeared with a baseball bat in hand. "Are you boys still okay?" he asked again.

"Just fine," Hank and I called out together.

"Pizza," Hector mumbled.

"Why don't you all slowly get up and see if you can walk around to us," Mom said, her eyes never leaving the monster.

"Roger that," Hank said. The two of us grabbed Hector and we slowly shuffled around the purple panty eater's backside and climbed over his tail that I noticed was thick with spots. The monster didn't even notice us. It continued to happily munch away on our wardrobe as we joined our parents by the doorway. Hector stumbled in front of us and Mom grabbed him before he toppled over.

"Why is Hector acting like that?" she asked, halfway between caring and frustration. "It looks like you were hit by a dump truck and haven't slept in three weeks."

"Um, we can explain, Mom," Hank said.

"I'm most certain you can. And will," she agreed, but was interrupted by a loud *BAUURRPPP!* We turned her eyes back to the thing in the center of the room.

"Did that thing just burp?" Mom asked in astonishment.

The crater-sized hole in the roof let the moonlight shine down on us. I could hear neighborhood dogs barking. The monster looked sideways at us and we all froze, but then he turned back to his meal.

"Hey, that was my favorite football shirt!" I called out and could feel my eye lasers heat up a little. Mom quickly covered my mouth.

"I'll buy you a new one," she whispered. "As soon as you re-pay your dad and I for the damage your new pet has made to the house."

"What? He's not our pet!" I responded. But Dad's eyes shifted to me, so I zipped my lips.

"It's gotta be like a hippo-elephant-ant mix," Hank commented. "Maybe his mom was a hippopotamus, his dad an ant, and his uncle an elephant."

"How does that make any sense?" I said. "Especially since none of those things eat football T-shirts."

Our conversation was cut short when we heard voices from outside the house.

"Herman? Henrietta?"

It was our neighbors, Mr. and Mrs. Davis. We could see the

beam from their flashlight through the window, bouncing on Mom's hydrangea bushes.

"Is everything okay? Mr. Davis was snoring away when we heard a loud crash . . . Mamma mia! What's that?" Mrs. Davis called out. Then we heard something hit the lawn.

Apparently, Mrs. Davis had never seen or probably smelled

a purple creature like the one still eating laundry like it was Halloween candy.

"Oh boy," Dad said, and he turned back down the hall. We all followed. Mom grabbed the closest pair of pants and slipped them on Hector. Then she wrapped her arms around him and carried him outside through the double doors.

Sure as slime on a slug, we found Mrs. Davis out cold, lying on the lawn. Mr. Davis was still standing, but not for long. Only a few seconds passed before his wide eyes rolled back, his wrinkled fingers released his cane, and thud, he landed on the lawn.

Dad leaned over and tapped their cheeks lightly. Mom was still holding up Hector with one arm. Both looked very concerned.

Within another minute, three more neighbors came calling through our fence, Ms. Okishi and the Woodhouses. I tried not to stare because Mrs. Woodhouse almost looked more monstrous than the purple giant in our room. At least fifty curlers were entangled in her hair and her entire face, except her eyes, was covered in green goo.

"Does Mrs. Woodhouse have a disease?" I whispered to Hank.

"I don't think so, little bro," he replied. "Old people do weird things to their faces at night."

"There's no such thing as witches, right?" I asked.

"I can't completely confirm that but Mrs. Woodhouse is too nice to be a witch. Plus she laughs more like a cute puppy than an evil witch," he said.

"Good point," I replied.

All three adults rushed over to my parents and the Davises. Then they caught a glimpse of our enormous purple visitor through the debris. Their eyes bulged.

Dad stopped trying to revive Mr. Davis, ran in the house, and grabbed his cell phone. Soon, I could hear the phone ringing but no one picked up. He tried once more, but still no answer.

"Hooligan Huddle!" Dad called.

On Dad's signal, both Hank and I joined my parents, interlinked arms, and brought our heads close. Mom pulled Hector in too even though he still smelled like rotten onions.

"Things are a bit out of control," he began, "but if we work as a team, we can figure this out. We need to revive Mr. and Mrs. Davis and figure out what to do with the monster." His eyebrows looked serious.

"I don't think he's a monster, Dad," I said.

"Not a monster? And what makes you think that?" he asked.

"Monsters eat brains, duh. He's eating our socks," I replied.

"He did attack Hector," Hank added.

"Is that how Hector got all these bumps and bruises?" Mom asked.

"Umm . . . well, no," Hank started. "We kinda dropped him a couple times, hit him with a longboard, and then ran his head into the window."

"You did *what*?" she shouted.

I interrupted, "The purple elephant fella just gave Hector a hug and he went all wet-noodle-y," I explained. "We had a hard time carrying him."

"A hug?" Dad asked.

"Yeah, like a big bear hug," confirmed Hank.

"I have a feeling there is a lot more to this story, but right now I need your help," he said.

He then pointed at Hank and me. "I need you two to race down to Doctor Dan's house and bring him here. Your mom and I need to be here to keep an eye on the Davises and the monst— the giant purple fella." Dad rolled his eyes.

"I want Doctor Dan to take a look at Hector as well," Mom said.

"Roger that," Hank replied.

"Yes, sir!" I echoed, and gave Dad a firm salute.

On three we all shouted, "Hooligan Huddle!" Hank and I found a new pair of shoes each and took off around the house at full speed. As we rounded the corner we heard Mom yell, "Watch out for cars!" I glanced at my football watch when it beeped. "How many cars does she think will be on the road at this time of night?" I asked.

"It's just a Mom thing," answered Hank. "Like I said, adults do weird stuff."

By the time Doctor Dan's house was in sight, both of us were out of breath. We Hooligans are good runners and are known to be the fastest around the bases on our baseball team, but sprinting four blocks over and three blocks up is a little too much. We slowed to a slight jog.

"Should we knock or go full-on doorbell?" I asked Hank.

"This is nothing short of a figgity-full-on emergency, little bro. Definitely full doorbell," he replied.

We were about to step up onto Doctor Dan's perfectly manicured lawn, when two very large shadows emerged from the bushes directly between us and the front door. The shadows were making ravenous zombie wolf sounds—*real* ravenous zombie wolf sounds. As the snarling got closer, we recognized them and their long pink tongues. The spiked collars and leashes they'd worn in the race earlier in the day were still attached and hung around their necks.

GGGU   UURR   RRR...

"Bugs and Bunny?!" I said in disbelief. "Seriously, we should be the feature story in *Lousy Luck Magazine!*"

Hank's eyebrows crept towards his nose.

"I don't see Rock anywhere—do you?" I said.

"Nope," Hank replied. "Looks like it's just the Hooligans versus the hounds."

"What do we do?" I asked. I wished I could shoot real lasers from my eyes because one of the options definitely would be frying these two blubber balls into crispy mutt muffins.

"Here's option number one," Hank said. He reached down, picked up a rock, and pitched it at the dogs. Only one of them flinched. The other caught it in his mouth and swallowed it.

"Holy Hepsibah!" I said. "THEY EAT ROCKS!"

"That's pretty ironic considering who their owner is," Hank said. "And he swallowed that thing whole!"

"They're gonna swallow us whole too if we don't do something quick," I panicked. "What's option two?"

"Run!" Hank yelled as he grabbed my arm and pulled me in the opposite direction. I have never hauled my buns faster.

I turned my head and saw the two dogs start after us. They were in attack mode.

Both Hank and I turned and sprinted across the street, looking for the first thing that might give us some protection, and saw an old pickup truck. As we ran around the passenger's side, I saw Hank glance inside. The Rottweilers were hot on our Hooligan heels. Thankfully, they were too fat to run very fast. Hank and I turned around the back of the truck and started running circles around the truck. After two times around, I yelled out to Hank, "I'm starting to feel like a gerbil!"

If Hector had been there he would have most definitely told me to eat a gerbil. So then I would have told him he smelled like gerbil toots.

"I know, hang in there, little bro! The driver's-side door is unlocked!"

On the third time around Hank reached for the handle but his hand slipped and he missed.

"No more missing, pretty please!" I yelled.

On the fourth time around he didn't miss. He grabbed the handle and swung the door open as we raced by. The dogs dodged the door and continued their pursuit.

"So the door is open—now what?" I asked.

"You're going to jump in and open the other door," Hank explained.

"What?" I yelled, breathing heavy.

Hank told me to trust him. So, on the next go-around I swung wide and shot like a missile onto the truck's bench seat. Sure as Hector smelled like sour pickles, gaping jaws and gnashing teeth followed me. When I kicked back, the beast grabbed ahold of my left shoe. In horror, I watched him rip it off my foot and eat it. What kind of animals were these?

I saw Hank run past again.

"Open the other door!" he hollered.

I pushed myself up and frantically scooted over and unlocked the passenger door. I wasn't sure if it was Bugs or Bunny still chasing Hank, I opened the door right after Hank passed by again. Smash! Bugs or Bunny collided with the door. The dog wobbled back and fell over.

"Sweet move, little bro!" called Hank, and he gave a mid-run fist pump.

But, still determined to sink his teeth into some Hooligan hind end, the dog got up again. His bark now sounded like he was snorkeling. He made another attempt around the truck, but lost  track of Hank. So he joined his partner in trying to get at me from the driver's side door. Hank came around and

I slipped out the passenger door. Both beasts couldn't seem to quite make it up into the truck cab, so we started taunting.

"C'mon you brainless rock-lovin' slobber-heads! Come and get us!" I said, as I pulled on my ears and rolled my eyes together.

Hank finally told them they were cuter than a couple of pink poodles and that seemed to do it. They both lunged forward through the cab with extra force. But before they could get to us . . . wham! I slammed the passenger door shut.

Hank hurried around and slammed shut the driver's-side door.

"Golden! Absolutely golden!" Hank hauled over and gave a superduper fist pump in the air.

I staggered back and collapsed on the grass nearby. I could hear Bugs and Bunny going frantic inside the pickup truck.

"Can I just please go to bed now?" I moaned. Hank lifted me up from behind. "Let's go, little bro.

We still have to get Doctor Dan."

"Oh yeah," I said, closing my eyes. "You go on without me. Even my pinky finger is exhausted."

"No way, Henry. We're a team, remember?" With that, he hoisted me up on my . . . well, one shoe and one sock.

Once we were across the street and on Doctor Dan's doorstep, we rang the bell and waited.

Nothing.

We rang it again. I looked at my watch. 11:47.

After a few moments and five doorbell rings later, we saw lights in the house flip on. The door opened slightly and we saw a sliver of Doctor Dan standing with a rifle in his hand. His eyes rested on us.

"Doctor Dan?" Hank started. "We're really, really, really sorry to be ringing your doorbell in the middle of the night, but there's an emergency at our house."

The door opened wider. "Is that you Hank? Henry?" The doctor asked.

"Yessir, Hank and Henry Hooligan," we answered.

"An emergency?" repeated Doctor Dan. "What kind of emergency? There are other doctors on call at the hospital, boys, you can call on one of them."

"Well . . . um, our dad told us to come and get you," I said. "You must be special."

He gave me an odd look.

"Our neighbors, the Davises, might be dead in our backyard and my brother is going crazy from alien poison," I said, choosing to leave out the part about the giant purple clothing eater.

Hank gave me an odd look as well.

"Two dead old people and alien poison? Sounds pretty serious, give me a second," Doctor Dan said. "Let me grab my bag and keys."

We waited out by his car until he came hustling out, still in his long blue robe. Both Hank and I climbed in the back and buckled up. As the car backed out of the driveway and turned down the street, something caught Doctor Dan's eye.

"What in tarnation is going on in Barney's truck?" he asked, primarily to himself. Hank and I glanced at each other and then out the window. The truck in question was rocking back and forth and rattling like a giant snake.

"Maybe your neighbor is wrestling a squirrel in his truck?" I suggested. Doctor Dan shot me another odd look through his rearview mirror and then we sped toward our house.

CHAPTER 7

Thunder and Lightning

By the time Hank and I had left and returned with Doctor Dan, dark clouds had gathered in the once-clear night sky. I felt a few raindrops on my ears. As we rounded the back of the house, a much larger group had gathered in the yard. Four more neighbors surrounded the Davises, but were also watching the giant purple pants-eating creature from Deadman's Hill: Mr. and Mrs. Brown, Mr. Zunderland and Sheriff Sherwood. The sheriff was on his phone.

Doctor Dan rushed over and slid his stethoscope onto Mrs. Davis's chest.

"Thanks for coming, Dan," we heard Dad say.

"I'm always happy to lend a hand," he replied as he jumped over to listen to Mr. Davis's chest as well.

"They both just, bam, dropped like a pair of unhinged doors," Dad continued. "We thought both had heart attacks."

"Well, it looks like they're simply unconscious," Doctor Dan said. "What in tarnation made them keel over rights here in y'all's backyard at this time of night? You have a coon problem?"

Doctor Dan hadn't noticed our purple visitor yet.

"It's a little bigger than a raccoon," Dad said, raising his pointer finger toward the house.

"Jumpin' jackrabbits!" Doctor Dan cried. His eyes opened wide and his eyebrows shot way up. "What in tarnation is *that* thing? You Hooligans have a new pet? Pretty *big* pet, if you ask me."

"We don't actually know what it is or where it came from," Mom cut in. "We just know where it landed."

YAK
YAK
YAK

"Actually, we do know where it came from!" I said. Hank gave me a look like I should be in mouse mode—in other words, not make a squeak. But the adults had asked.

"And where is that?" Dad prompted.

"Umm . . . Deadman's Hill," I continued. "It lives in the rocks up there."

Mom's eyes bored into Hank. "Did you three go back up that hill tonight?"

Before we could respond we heard Hector mumble.

"Is Hector the one with alien poison?" Doctor Dan asked.

"Yessir," I said. "He got hugged by the big purple fella, and since then, all he wants is pizza."

"Let me have a look-see," Doctor Dan said, and he dropped to one knee on the wet grass.

He pulled out the stethoscope thing, listened, then shone a light in Hector's eyes. Then he opened up Hector's mouth. From inside, Doctor Dan pulled two huge globs of purple goop dripping with drool.

"You'll not be eatin' pizza if you're hoarding purple slime in your yapper," he said.

Hector's eyes came to life a little more. "Bag of hair! That was *disgusting*!" he said.

"You mean you've had that stuff in your mouth this whole time?" asked Hank.

"Yeah!" Hector complained. "When the people eater grabbed

me, my face went straight into his chest. I was about to yell when I got a mouthful of monster."

"You ate some of it?" I asked. "That's worse than holding goat guts in your mouth!"

Hector said I should gobble goat guts.

I smiled. I was glad he was getting better.

Mom pulled Hector closer. "Oh, are you feeling better, Hector Wector?" She sometimes called him that, which drove him crazy.

He was still not back to normal, but said, "Yeah, I think so. But my tongue still feels like a puffy marshmallow."

As we turned our attention to Hector, the rain had gotten heavier. In the distance we heard thunder, too. Mom had been praying for rain so her petunias would grow. But she probably hadn't considered that there would be an enormous hole in our roof.

The neighbors in our yard weren't quite sure what to do. The Davises were still on the lawn being watered by the rain. Until FLASH! The night sky lit up. Two seconds later, a crash of thunder boomed overhead. BAM! And just then, Mr. and Mrs. Davis shot back upright, their eyes as wide as owls.

"Well, that's one way to do the trick," Doctor Dan said. "Let's get these ol' hoots inside!"

Dad hurried over to help them up as well. Mr. Davis must have been dreaming, because he started swinging his cane around like a lightsaber and yelling at some monster to leave his tomato plants alone. "To the death!" he cried.

The Woodhouses, Ms. Okishi, and the others asked if we knew what we were going to do about the creature in our house. Chances were he was still sitting in our bedroom eating. Hopefully it had finished off all my hand-me-downs by now.

I picked my way through the house and stepped around the rubble for a better look at the big fella. His body was turned away from me but his sides were still moving in and out. In and out. Then I realized he had stopped eating—he'd fallen alseep! I could see one of his eyes was shut.

"Dad, Dad!" I called quietly. "I think he's asleep."

After helping the Davises inside, Dad cautiously worked his way over to me, scolding me for getting so close. Another bolt of lightning flared down the street. The thunder was so loud we all covered our ears. But the big fella's eyes remained closed and his breathing was strong but slow.

"You're right, son," Dad agreed. "It's out like a light. This is good. It should be much easier for the animal control people to nab it."

"What?" I said. "Animal control people?"

"Sheriff Sherwood contacted a specially trained team from the animal control agency, and they're on their way," he continued.

This news didn't sound very golden to me. Sure, the big fella had caused us to lose the race, had just about smothered Hector to death, had eaten all our clothes, caved in our roof, and smelled worse than old-man rotten-egg toots, but the idea of seeing it captured in a net or cage just seemed not so cool. And it wasn't like it had attacked us. And to be honest, the smell was hardly noticeable anymore.

But before I could dwell on it any longer, everyone outside began shouting. We looked up at the dark sky and noticed a thick black trail of smoke flowing upward into the rain and stormy clouds.

"Fire!"

CHAPTER 8
Smoke and Fire

With the purple giant still snoozing away, everyone raced around to the front of the house. Sure as a fish has guts, red and yellow flames lit up the street four doors down at the Pickerings' house. Their house was the only other one on our street with kids our age.

"Come on!" Dad yelled to Doctor Dan, and bolted down the street. Mom kicked off her slippers and took off as well. A little known fact about my mom is this: She holds the Skunkerton High School record in the 100-meter dash, and can still move faster than a cheetah with jet boosters.

The rest of us followed a bit more slowly. More neighbors emerged from their homes and I could see Lady Lopez on the phone. Hopefully, she wasn't ordering a pizza. I'm just saying—I always see the Domino's Pizza delivery guy at her house.

I watched as Mom stopped next to her and asked if the fire department was on their way. Lady Lopez nodded. But Dad didn't stop. He ran full speed straight to the front door and lowered his shoulder. CRASH! The blue door came off its hinges. Wow, I didn't see that coming. Coolest. Dad. Ever.

"You see, that's what I'm talking about. If we didn't have

doors, Dad wouldn't have had to bust his shoulder to get inside," Hector said.

Thirty seconds later Mrs. Pickering stumbled out, holding their wailing baby and followed by her two twin sons. Dad came out too, carrying four-year-old Patrick on his back. Dad's eyebrows had been singed off, so if they were up or down we couldn't tell.

"Penny is still in there!" Mrs. Pickering called. "I couldn't find her!"

Dad sat Patrick down and rushed to enter the house again, but was instantly pushed back by an enormous wall of flames.

"I can't get past!" he called as he ran around the side of the house. By this time the entire neighborhood had gathered in the street. Mom had her arms around Mrs. Pickering, both pairs of eyes fixed on the blaze. Dad emerged around the other side.

"I can't get in!" he called.

From above, we heard a shout, "Mamma!"

It was Penny. She was trapped. It was just like a movie but not. My heart was racing a million-billion-gazillion beats a second. Girls are gross and have cooties, but I always got put next to Penny for class pictures and nothing has rubbed off on me yet. In fact, if I had a club, she would be the only girl I might let join because her hair smells like peaches. And all of us Hooligans love peaches; especially peaches with cottage cheese.

We heard her cry again and could see Penny's peachy hair in the attic window. Smoke was pouring out as well. The only thing I could think of was saving Penny. If only I had bionic fireproof skin. I could be a hero like in the movies.

The sirens from the fire engines could be heard in the distance, but they were still a few minutes away. The Pickerings' neighbor, Mr. Canada, came running with a ladder and threw it up against the house, but it was too short. Tears were running down Mrs. Pickering's face. I looked around at everyone, feeling frantic and helpless when all of a sudden my eyes landed on the answer.

"Hank, look!" I shouted. He spotted it as well and without a word we both bolted across the yard. Hector connected the dots and made his way over as best he could. Next thing I know, both Mom and Dad were there as well. "It's worth a try boys!" Dad said to us. "One, two, three, Hooligan Hoist!" Spread out evenly around the Pickering's backyard trampoline, we lifted the trampoline and quickly carried it over and set it directly beneath Penny.

We all raised our chins and yelled, "Jump! Jump!"

Penny was coughing uncontrollably in the smoke, but she looked down and saw the trampoline. Climbing up on the windowsill, she stalled. We could see the fear in her face.

"She's not going to jump, Dad!" I yelled over. "What else can we do?"

I had barely gotten the question out when out of nowhere a huge purple mass bounded past my left ear, leaped onto the trampoline, and launched itself into the air. The monster from Deadman's Hill reached the second story and slammed his hands into the walls. Then he pulled himself up the side. He must have been half salamander or maybe related to King Kong with the way he climbed.

The whole neighborhood was in a trance. They watched as the giant monster with two antennae and a huge tail made his way up to the attic window. Penny was still sobbing uncontrollably, but now I wasn't sure if it was out of fear of burning to death or being eaten by a ginormous purple monster. Either way, she had little choice. Wide-eyed and cautious she backed into the smoky attic, but a purple arm ripped off the window and reached in after her. Still crying at the top of her lungs, Penny was pulled out and held by one leg, upside down, dangling three stories up.

A unified gasp came from the entire crowd.

"He's probably just after her PJs!" Hector said.

With a swing of his arm, the giant flung Penny head over heels into the air.

Mrs. Chow put her hand to her head and dropped on the lawn in front of us. That made three people I'd seen pass out tonight.

All our hearts stopped as we watched Penny spin high in the air in slow motion. The creature leaped from the house, landed on a rhododendron bush, and caught Penny with one arm. It looked like a circus act.

"Now that was golden!" Hank said.

"How far up did he just jump from?" I asked in amazement.

"What a show-off," Hector said.

"Well, it's a pretty good show-off, if you ask me," I replied. "It's better than your two-minute handstands."

"I bet you a gazillion dollars that purple dude couldn't do a handstand for one second," Hector shot back.

The giant stepped away from the burning house and it looked like it was sweating or something. It sat Penny down and Mrs. Pickering ran to her daughter. She wrapped Penny up in a huge hug.

All the rest of us just stood there, not sure what to look at: the burning house, the giant monster hero, or Penny and her mom. I was looking at the hero, but I might have glanced over at Penny's peachy hair, too. It was a little singed on one side.

"Here they come!" Hank yelled, pointing down the street.

A bright red fire engine arrived and the crowd gave way to a huge hose and five firefighters. According to my watch it took seven minutes and thirty-five seconds for them to arrive. It felt like it had been seven hours.

Each fireman jumped out and went to work. As they took their positions on the hose, one finally saw the giant monster still standing on the front lawn. His eyebrows shot up and his mouth dropped open. He tripped over the hose and fell into the firefighter in front of him. Like dominos, all five firemen tumbled to the ground just as forty-four cubic centimeters of water burst from the nozzle.

"Holy bag of hair!" Hector yelled. "Look out!"

We turned and hauled buns with the rest of the neighbor-hood! Everyone darted in different directions as we tried to avoid the swelling fire hose that had come to life. It writhed back and forth like an angry snake, spewing water in all directions.

The firemen climbed to their feet to try to tame the hose, but the water pressure was so strong that each firefighter couldn't hold it alone. After two were blasted in the face and knocked to the ground, our purple hero stepped over, grabbed the hose, and shoved the end into his mouth with one hand.

"Dude, that thing can stuff it and chug it," Hank said.

"No kidding," I replied. "I call he's on my team for the ham-dog hoedown." That's our famous hamdog eating contest.

"He'd probably mistake your face for a hamdog and eat it, too," Hector added.

"Your brain is made of hamdog leftovers," I shot back.

Done quenching his thirst, the monster pulled the hose from his mouth and held it in one purple paw. Water sprayed straight up into the night sky, adding to the rain. The monster scanned the stunned crowd of people staring back at it. The firemen, now back on their feet, weren't sure how exactly to get their hose back.

"Should we try to tackle it?" I heard one fireman say.

"Maybe we can wrap him up in the other hoses?" another whispered.

Then a gruff old voice yelled from the crowd, "Well, don't just stand there, you big fat grape! Put the fire out!" It was Old Man Otts, and as he yelled, he pointed at the burning house. A few more voices echoed the command.

"Put the fire out!"

Soon we were all chanting like we were at a high school football game: "PUT! THE! FIRE! OUT!"

At first the creature stepped back and looked a little afraid, but I could see his eyes follow our pointing fingers to the house. Its eyebrows lifted and it shifted the huge stream of water toward the fire. The entire crowd shouted in approval and the big guy got a bunch of thumbs-ups. The firefighters ran around and grabbed three smaller hoses and cranked on the water. Within five minutes the fire was under control, thanks to the rain, five firemen and, of course, one giant purple monster.

Dad was standing next to Hank, Hector, and me, his hand on my shoulder. I looked up at him and asked, "So, are the animal catcher people still coming to wrap him up in a giant net or cage or something?"

Dad looked down at me. "Yep. Sheriff Sherwood said they should be here shortly."

"Dad, I don't think that's a very golden idea. We have no idea what it really is, which means they'll probably strap it down in some underground lab, poke it with a whole bunch of needles, and shove tubes up its nose."

"How can they do that?" Hector chimed in. "It doesn't even have a nose."

"I agree with Henry," Hank added. "This purple dude just rescued Penny and is now a volunteer fireman. How can we turn him over to a bunch of crazy-haired scientists? If anything, we should be putting money in his boot."

"Maybe they'll just stuff it and hang it in a museum," Hector said. "Then you two can go visit your precious overgrown eggplant whenever you want."

"Settle down, boys," Dad broke in. "I don't see any other

option. You're correct that we don't know what it is. Therefore, we don't know what it can—or will—do."

"Come on, Dad! Sure, he caved in our roof, but the only thing he's attacked was our closet."

"It attacked me, remember?" Hector blurted out.

"No, it hugged you," Hank said. "And besides, you're fine, now that you hacked up that purple hairball."

"Boys, I have no idea what we'd do with a creature like that," Dad said. "It's not like a stray cat that you can just feed milk to on your back porch."

"Yes, we can!" I said. "We'll just feed it socks instead. Mom has a huge mound of mismatches she's always adding to."

"Awesome idea, Dad," Hank blurted. "It lives up on Deadman's Hill, but it can come down every night and we'll feed it."

"Come on, Dad, come on!" I argued again. "We can't let it be captured. Can you imagine living in a cage for the rest of your life, being injected with all sorts of weird green and red bubbling liquids every day?"

"Maybe if it was Jell-O," he smirked, his missing eyebrows shooting up. But then they both went down and I could see Dad was really thinking about this now. He called Mom over and they stepped aside to discuss our proposition.

"Hooligan Huddle," Dad called a few seconds later. Once we were huddled in a circle, Dad said, "Okay, your mom and I agree that the monster has been quite helpful and hasn't eaten any brains—yet. It doesn't seem to be overly threatening, but there is no way we can hide something like that. I'm sorry, boys, unfortunately we have to let it go. Too many people have seen it. Someone is bound to turn it in anyway. "

"Not if I can help it!" Hank said. "I have an idea." He broke away and hauled buns to the fire truck. Inside, he found the loudspeaker the firemen use to tell everyone to "clear

the area," and he climbed up on top of the truck and flipped the switch.

"Fellow residents of Shoemaker Street, can I have your attention please!" he began. "I'm Hank Hooligan."

Everyone looked up and found Hank.

"Hey! Son, you gotta get down from there!" one of the fireman shouted.

But Hank continued: "I want to argue in behalf of the big purple fella. Right now, there are government mad-scientist animal control people on their way to take him away and inject him with deadly toxic-waste Jell-O."

Hank never lied, but he did have this thing for stretching the truth a little.

"We Hooligans feel that this is a big mistake. It hasn't hurt anyone, but it did save Penny's life and as we all saw it helped us put the fire out and keep our neighborhood safe. I mean, if it had hurt any of us I could see turning it in, but that's not the case. If we let it be taken away, there is no doubt they will keep it locked up in some secret facility in the desert, performing daily tests and experiments. The Hooligan family is willing to take responsibility and feed our purple visitor. All we are asking is that no one here turns it in."

The crowd burst to life with chatter. I could hear Old Man Otts grumbling loudly behind us, but most seemed to be in agreement. One of the firemen had made his way up on top of the truck and was kneeling beside Hank trying to convince him to come down. But Hank just fired the loudspeaker back up.

"So, what do you say? If you're in, please raise your thumb high up into the air."

I raised my thumb and look around. Unbelievably, everyone was following Hank's lead, including the firemen. Everyone except Hector, that is—he had his thumb pointed sideways.

"Come on, Hector," I nudged him. "We're doing the right thing. We'll make sure he doesn't give you any more hugs."

"Go lick a slug," he replied and dropped his hand.

He was in. Kind of.

CHAPTER 9

Smokey the Bear

With everyone in agreement, Hank handed the loudspeaker to the fireman and climbed down.

Dad made his way over to Sheriff Sherwood.

"You sure you're good with this, sheriff?" Dad asked.

"The boy's got a point. I'm sure there's some small print somewhere that requires me to turn the thing in, but relative to the kind of invading space aliens you see in the movies, it seems pretty darn harmless. Plus, I've lost my reading glasses. I might eat my words in the coming days, but we'll give it a shot. You just gotta get it gone pronto. The agency should be here within fifteen minutes."

"Ten-four," Dad said.

"Now what?" Hector asked, rolling his eyes.

"We have to somehow get the big fella back up to Deadman's Hill," I said.

"And let me guess, we Hooligans are just going to boy-scout carry it back up the hill?" Hector griped.

Dad intervened, "We can use the Big Banana." That's Dad's old yellow truck he got from Grandpa. He drove it in the town parade one year decorated as a banana. Dad loves bananas on his cereal, too, so it seemed to fit.

"Can we lure it in with some washcloths?" Mom asked. "We're running out of socks."

"Worth a try," Dad said. "It likes eating boys' dirty clothes, why not old rags? Henry, come with me and we'll grab some garage rags and then fire up the Big Banana."

"I'll get the firemen to shut down the big fella's hose," Hank said.

While running back to the house, I noticed the storm had shifted a bit. It was raining much less.

At the house, Dad and I found a bundle of rags and jumped into the Big Banana. Even with a little delay as the Banana sputtered to life, according to my watch, we pulled back in front of the Pickerings' house in four minutes and twenty-eight seconds.

"So how do we do this?" I asked as Dad and I pulled handfuls of old rags out of the Banana.

"Why don't you just run up and grab its tail and drag it on over?" suggested Hector. "Since you think it's so cute and cuddly, I'm sure it will come along purring like a kitten."

"I've got a better idea. Let's hang you on a stick and use you as bait," I shot back. "You know you're his favorite. Maybe he'll even share some more of his skin with you."

"Eat rotten toe skin yourself," Hector spit back.

Dad dropped the tailgate on the truck and then approached the giant, cautiously holding up the rags. The purple creature turned and looked straight at him. Its mouth dropped open and we could see its round teeth and green tongue. But it didn't budge. Dad tossed a couple rags at its feet. I could hear the crowd of neighbors, still very much present, whispering nervously. Dad threw the rest of the rags over. The monster picked up a couple and tossed them in his mouth but still didn't move.

My watch beeped. One o'clock in the morning. "We gotta think of something quick," I said. The sheriff had given us fifteen minutes and that had been at twelve forty-five.

"Maybe we should just try to lasso it with the ropes in the back of the truck and drag it out of here?" Hank said. "I know it's a less-than-golden idea, but it's better than letting the mad doctors at it."

I strained my brain. "Think. Think. Think. Think, think,

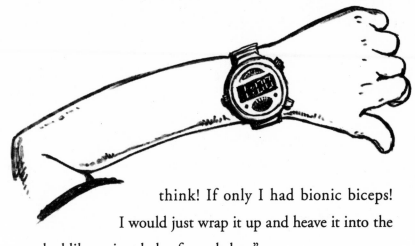

think! If only I had bionic biceps!
I would just wrap it up and heave it into the
bed like a giant bale of purple hay."

My brain was being as useful as a dead engine in a drag race
when two sets of headlights turned the corner at the far end of
the street, about two football fields away.

"It's the animal control agency people!" Hank called.

"Oh, bag of hair!" Hector said with an irritated voice behind
me.

I turned in time to see him climb into the back of the truck.
He kicked off his shoes and pulled off his socks. "Hey, you big
creepy eggplant! Come and get me!"

And sure as slime on a slug, that was just what happened. The
giant monster dropped the deflated hose, lumbered over to the
truck, and climbed into the bed. Hector was trying to be brave,
but his eyebrows had shot way up on his forehead. What was he
thinking? I had totally been kidding about using him as bait.

Hector had his two long socks held up high.

"Alright!" we heard him call. "It's in the truck! Let's get moving!"

Mom, Dad, and the sheriff were beside the truck.

"Will you be okay, Hector Wector?" Mom asked.

"I'm sacrificing myself, my socks, and maybe the rest of my clothes to save this giant purple ant. Can we PLEASE haul some buns?" he blurted.

The big fella stooped down and plucked one sock from Hector's hand and

opened its mouth. Then he fell back on his tail. The truck bounced with the weight and the headlights pointed up in the air. Jumping in the passenger side of the truck, Hank yelled, "Come on, Dad! Let's make like a bakery truck!"

Dad got a nod from Mom and revved the engine. With a jerk, the Big Banana shot off toward Deadman's Hill, leaving behind a trail of smoke. I waved.

Nine seconds

after they had sped around the corner, two black vans pulled up next to the fire truck and the Pickerings' house. Three men and a woman climbed out into the light rain and scanned the scene. They had on dark uniforms like park rangers, and each was wearing Smokey-the-Bear hats and sunglasses.

Why are they wearing sunglasses at night? I asked myself. *I bet they shoot lasers from their eyes and the only thing stopping them from destroying everything in sight are those sunglasses. Just like Cyclops from X-Men.* That was really the only logical explanation.

Sheriff Sherwood made his way over and greeted them.

"No time for chitchat, Sheriff," I heard the woman say with a snarl. "Where's the beast that caused this mayhem? I can't wait to set my eyes on this giant purple marshmallow hippo that can stand on two legs. Isn't that how you described it?"

"Yes, ma'am. Well . . . uh, actually . . . we might have mischaracterized the intruder, it being night and all. We're pretty

sure it was a bear, a very large bear. Probably a grizzly," Sheriff Sherwood explained. "In the dark the creature didn't look all that recognizable. But after a while we decided it was a bear."

"You *decided* it was a bear? Or *is* it a bear?" the woman growled, eyebrows now uneven.

"Oh, uh, we're darn sure it was a bear," the sheriff said, chuckling a little and pulling up on his belt.

"You said it was purple. So what you saw was a giant purple grizzly bear?"

"Well, ma'am, it must have just been a trick of the neighborhood lights and maybe the lightning. Turns out it was just a regular ol' brown color when we got a better look-see. Plus, I'm totally colorblind anyhow!" he said with another light chuckle.

She ground her teeth. "Then where might this large, um, *bear* be?" she asked.

"Well, ma'am, it has fled the scene, actually. Probably gone on home to get a little honey for dinner, would be my guess."

"Sheriff, you do know that a large grizzly bear in this part of the country is highly, highly unlikely, don't you?" the woman continued, her nose scrunching. "If this creature is indeed what you say it is, it would be a very long way from any sort of home *or* honey."

"Well, ain't that good!" Sheriff Sherwood said. "Darn good chance it'll be out of our hair then."

"No, actually, this means it most likely will roam your streets in search of tasty snacks, like big-eared kindergartners. I have no doubt this is why it was here tonight."

Then a voice called from the Pickerings' front lawn.

"Chief, looks like the animal's print is here," one of the guys still wearing his sunglasses said. He was kneeling down, looking at two of the giant purple fella's footprints in the lawn.

Everyone ran over to examine the footprint.

"Looks like a bear print to me!" Sheriff Sherwood said.

"That's an odd-shaped bear print," the woman replied.

"No, it ain't. If anyone should be able to identify Smokey-the-Bear's footprint it should be you three—y'all have the same hats!" the sheriff said, laughing at his own joke.

The woman just scowled back at him, then the three of them huddled and began talking in low voices. I watched them for a moment then got bored.

Nobody had returned to their houses since the fire started. Doctor Dan had revived the woman who had fainted. Walking behind them, I noticed a boy handing out leaflets. He was all dressed in black and had his back toward me. But after giving a paper to Mrs. Woodhouse, he turned in my direction. I definitely knew him. It was Rock, the old-lady lip-kisser.

"What in holy Hepsibah's name is he doing here? Especially in the middle of the night?" I said under my breath. Rumor had it that his house was on the other side of the railroad tracks, which was on the other side of Bubba's Burger Barn, which was on the other side of the river, which was on the other side of Deadman's Hill. Even if he had bionic eyes and ears, there was no way he saw the fire or heard the commotion from his house.

I tracked him as he moved from person to person, until he was two people away from me. When our eyes connected, his eyebrows crawled down, way down. I swore I heard a low snarl escape his mouth. For a long moment, we just stared at each other. No words were exchanged. I felt my eye lasers heating up. Then he slowly turned and continued with his handouts. Out of the corner of my eye I glimpsed one of Rock's papers stuck to the side of the fire truck wheel, wet, torn, and flapping slightly in the wind. If I had bionic extendable arms I could have grabbed it and not moved, but I didn't yet, so I made my way over and peeled it off the tire.

The word "MISSING" was written across the top and a picture of two large black dogs was printed in the middle. Rock's name was on the bottom with a phone number.

I looked up. The big bully had moved from the crowd and was stapling three fliers to a telephone pole. I walked over, debating if I should tell him that his two brainless beasts were trapped in a rusty old truck. No. Yes? Honestly, I would have preferred to have left them there for . . . oh, until the earth was invaded by UFOs and aliens ate them for dinner.

Then Mom's words echoed in my mind. "Henry Hooligan, you treat people how you want them to treat you, regardless of who they are."

"But it's Rock!" I argued with Mom's voice in my head.

When Rock turned, his eyes were pinkish and he looked horrible, like he'd been up all night. Like me, he was wet from the rain and a little dirty, too.

"If you keep staring at me," he began, "I'm going to scramble your brains and eat them with ketchup."

"Yuck," I thought. Everyone in my family liked ketchup on their scrambled eggs. It only made me want to gag. And only someone with a scrambled-egg brain would think of that.

"Lost something?" I asked, ignoring his threat. "Or two somethings?"

He glared at me almost like he had bionic eye lasers himself. I wondered if our eye lasers collided in midair, who would win?

"Your precious slime balls not come home to cuddle with you last night?" I continued.

"**NONE OF YOUR BEESWAX**," Rock replied, gritting his teeth.

"What if I told you I know where your drool-face mutts are?"

One of Rock's eyebrows twitched a little and he took two steps closer to me. Remembering that Hank and Hector weren't here, and Rock was four times bigger than me, a hint of nervousness ran up my spine. Maybe I should cool the smart talk a little.

In a deep, slow voice Rock said, "I'm listening."

I hesitated a moment, thinking. "What would I get in return for their location?" I felt like a secret agent negotiating with a supervillain.

Rock's eyebrows narrowed even more. Clearly his scrambled-egg brain was struggling. "I will not collect on my race winnings," he muttered.

"Wait. What? Hold your horses," I said. "You think you *won* our race?"

"You lost, so that means I won," he spit back. "You hooli-babies shot right off the track; an automatic disqualification."

He has a point, I thought. This was not good. And because we were ahead of him, we didn't see what happened after soaring off into Grasshopper Acres. There was no way he made it around the big purple creature, though. Argh! If only I had glanced in the rearview mirror! Or better yet, if I had a third bionic eye in the back of my head, I would have been able to see everything that had happened.

"Didn't you swerve off the road, too?" I asked. "You didn't run into that big, um, purple thing, did you?"

"None of your beeswax," he answered.

"What happened, then?" I tried again. "Something had to have happened or your precious walrus-mutts wouldn't have run off."

"If you really know where Bugs and Bunny are, you have three seconds to tell me, or I take back my offer and start breaking hooli-things. And since you're the only hooli-baby here . . ."

I honestly didn't know what to say. So I gave in to the old-lady lip-kisser. Plus, the longer his monsters were in the truck, the greater chance there was they'd leave some presents on the seat for the truck's owner.

"They may or may not be locked in an old truck on Doctor Dan's street. It's two streets over that way," I point.

"An old truck?" Rock's one eyebrow shot up. "How'd they get locked in an old truck?"

"NONE OF YOUR BEESWAX."

• • •

As Rock left I noticed he was limping. He was in a hurry so I didn't get to ask why he was walking like a weasel with a wedgie.

Mom came over and put her arm around me.

"Your dad just called me, and they're on their way back," she said. "Things look under control out here. Let's get you inside, you look like a drowned muskrat—and I'm sure I do, too."

"What about Penny and her family?" I asked.

"They're headed to her uncle's house on the other side of town," she replied.

My football watch beeped. Three in the morning. I couldn't believe I'd been up almost all night! I had always wondered what it would feel like. Turns out, it felt kind of noodle-y. I mean, my body felt like a wet noodle, all out of energy and wet from the rain.

"This day has been a doozy and left me a little dizzy. Let's get you to bed," Mom said.

"Bed sounds good. But um, Mom, I don't have a bedroom anymore," I replied.

"You're right. That monster did a number on the house, didn't he?" Mom said with a slight frown.

"Mom, he's not a monster," I reminded her. "He's just a unique breed of . . . well, something."

One of her eyebrows shot up as if she wasn't quite sure of that.

"You boys will have to crash in the TV room for a while until we can get things back together," she said.

"Can we make a fort?" I asked.

"A fort? Your bedroom is in shambles and you want a fort?" she started. "You never stop with the adventures, do you?"

"No, ma'am!" I said. "Our motto is 'Do a Good Adventure Daily.'"

"Sounds similar to the Boy Scout motto," she said.

"Yeah, Hank says it's just adapted a little to suit our personal style," I explained.

Once inside, I changed out of my wet clothes. Mom found my favorite blanket and pillow. Both had been lucky enough to be in the washer and escaped the destruction earlier in the night.

"I know we're all tuckered out," Mom said, "but don't forget your prayers."

"Roger that," I said.

I was determined to be awake when the Big Banana pulled in, but the lights went out the instant my third-grade head hit the pillow.

CHAPTER 10

What Stinks?

When my lights came back on again, sunshine was peeking through the windows and my neck hurt. I must not have moved an inch because I woke up still on my knees, hands together under my chest, head on the pillow, and bum stuck up in the air.

I turned my head and met Hector's nose. He was dead asleep with his mouth wide open. Man-o-man, his breath stunk! I was tempted to tape his eyelids shut just because that would be awesome funny.

My watch beeped, so I sat up. Eleven-thirty in the morning. It looked like Hank had slept on the other side of Hector, but he was long gone. I jumped up and scooted into the kitchen. Nobody was there. I heard Dad and Mom talking down the hall outside our bedroom—or what was left of it. They had a huge fan blowing into the room trying to dry things out. A big tarp covered the hole in the roof.

"So, where's the big fella?" I asked right off the bat.

"Good morning, dear," Mom said with a half-smile. It was obvious she was still worn out and not thrilled about the condition of our house.

"So, where's the big fella?" I said again.

"Hopefully, still on Deadman's Hill," Dad said. He looked funny without eyebrows and half of his hair singed from the fire. I never thought eyebrows were that important, but when they're gone you end up looking like something from another planet.

"How'd you get him out of the truck?" I continued.

"Hector performed his magic again," Dad said. "He waited to give up the second sock until he hopped out. The purple monstrosity followed along like a puppy. We threw the rest of the rags and an old flannel shirt I had in the truck over the barricades. It must love flannel, 'cause I'd bet my britches I heard it say 'Yum!' with its first bite."

"It can talk?" I asked.

"I don't know," Dad said. "I just heard something that sounded like a deep 'Yum!'"

"So will it be safe up there?" I asked.

"Not completely sure—there were a lot of people that witnessed the scene last night," Dad said. "I'm stunned everyone there actually agreed to keep it from the animal control agency."

"My thumb was sideways," a voice said from behind me.

Hector was awake and had punk rocker hair.

"How could anyone have turned it in after it saved Penny?" I asked.

"You should have jumped up there and rescued her," Hector said. "Then she would have called you her hero and smooched you."

"**GO SMOOCH SOME SEAWEED**," I shot back.

"That would be better than smooching Penny Pickering!" Hector said.

"Well, if there is a good place to hide him, it is up on Deadman's Hill. Who knows how long he's been up there?" Dad added. "Most stay away from it because of the old stories about that hill."

"What stories?" Mom asked, snatching the question right out of my mouth.

Since Dad grew up here in Skunkerton, the town with the nation's highest skunk population, he knows most everybody and everything about it.

"Well, Deadman's Hill got its name from an old tale. Supposedly, seven men died up on that hill a long time ago. As the stories go, they were some of the first settlers here and fought off some sort of space monster invasion."

My eyebrows popped up. So did Mom's, but only one of Hector's jumped.

"Space monster invasion?" I blurted out.

"Yeah, supposedly, the men and monsters battled for an entire day. The settlers won but just as the last invader went down, it shot out some sort of cosmic dust from its body. All seven men were poisoned and staggered aimlessly down the hill. When they reached the bottom, they dropped dead. Years later the town received a government grant to build a space observatory up there, but they only completed the road before most of the construction workers came down with a strange sickness, so they blocked off the road and canceled the project."

I could tell Hector was thinking the exact same thing I was. We'd been up and down that hill many times this summer. I felt my throat swelling a little, and my stomach gurgled, but that could have been because I hadn't had breakfast yet.

"But I played on that hill as a boy with my friends, and there's nothing wrong with me," Dad continued. A random muscle in his neck jumped.

"You sure about that?" Hector asked.

Mom put her hand on Dad's shoulder. "Let's get some breakfast, boys. How about hash browns?"

At the mention of our favorite food, everyone smiled and eyebrows went up. Well, except for Dad's, since the fire had erased them the night before.

We all moved back into the kitchen, though I was still poking at my throat to gauge how easy it was to swallow. I hoped I hadn't been poisoned by alien toxins.

I grabbed some potatoes from the pantry and volunteered to grate them into the skillet.

Hector grabbed the dishes and began to set the table. "I've had enough of that hill," he said. "And enough of that creature, whatever it is. The taste of his skin is still on my tongue and I've brushed my teeth nine times."

"Well, try a few more times then," Dad said. "But do it quick, because the three of you are expected at the Flannigans' in about thirty minutes. We need to eat fast."

All three of us boys let out a long groan. I had almost forgotten that we still had to fix the mess we'd caused with our Hooligan Hasher.

Hector was especially grumpy about it. "If that big, fat, purple pomegranate hadn't gotten in our way, we would have stayed on the track, won the race, and not had to spend the last of our summer fixing a fence and flowers and birdbath and mailbox and door!"

If only I had a bionic brain, I thought. *I could invent a time machine and we could redo the race.*

It was a great thought but until that happened, it looked like we'd have to fix this mess the old-fashioned way.

So after a quick round of hash browns, we hopped in the Big Banana and headed down to the Flannigans'.

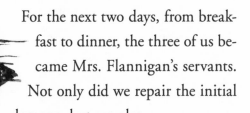

• • •

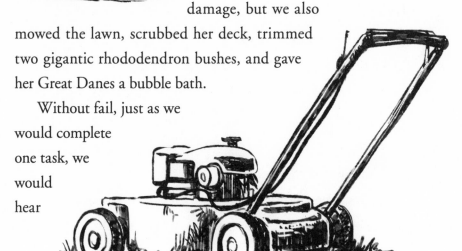

For the next two days, from breakfast to dinner, the three of us became Mrs. Flannigan's servants. Not only did we repair the initial damage, but we also mowed the lawn, scrubbed her deck, trimmed two gigantic rhododendron bushes, and gave her Great Danes a bubble bath.

Without fail, just as we would complete one task, we would hear her call in a light, airy voice, "Oh boys, since you caused such a ruckus and I know you want to redeem yourselves from being such hooligans—though I'm not sure that is entirely possible since your last name *is* Hooligan—I have just a few more things you could help me with."

And to top it all off, she fed us peanut butter and carrot sandwiches with tomato juice for lunch. Yuck.

• • •

At breakfast on the third day Hector blurted out, "I can't work for Mrs. Flannigan another second. She's driving me crazy! I'd rather hug that monster again ten more times than go back over there."

"Well, your wish might come true," Mom said. "Mrs. Flannigan called earlier and said she had to leave town today. She won't return until next week."

All three of us cried out, "*GOLDEN!*"

"However, your dad and I need to run to the hardware store for some more materials to fix your room, so I'll be sure to leave a nice list of items for you to work on here while we're out."

"Not golden," we moaned.

By the time Mom and Dad pulled out of the driveway, we each had a chore list in our pockets.

The three of us sat back down at the table and poured another bowl of cereal. My football watch beeped—nine in the morning.

"Anyone want to trade loading the dishwasher for something else?" I asked.

Hector scrunched his nose. "I'll trade you for cleaning the toilets."

There are only two toilets compared to a whole sink full of dishes. I was about to take the deal when the stench of giant purple creature hit my nose. Spinning, I found the big fella's face filling our half-open back window!

"Bag of hair!" Hector shouted. "Purple just passed brown on my list of the ugliest colors."

We all pinched our noses and froze. Neither of us moved an inch, including the purple monster.

"Well, this is just fantastic," Hector spouted, sounding like a duck. "How are we going to get rid of it? Mom put all the surviving socks in the washing machine."

We sat there staring at the purple face in the window for a few moments. "There's gotta be another solution," Hank quacked. "Something else it likes. Something else we can lure him back to Deadman's Hill with. Just think. Think."

I suggested trying milk. "We know it drinks water—maybe it would like milk? Or, better yet, orange juice?"

"I don't have any orange juice made up," Hank said. "Better stick with the milk."

"It's not a little kitty," Hector said.

"How do you know? Maybe it's just an undiscovered breed of kitty," I said. "Come on, it's worth a try."

"No kittens have antennae on their heads," Hector pointed out. "And if they did, they'd be biologically classified as insects."

So Hank poured a bowl of milk and slipped it out the back sliding glass door onto the porch step. He closed and locked the door—though I'm sure if the big fella wanted to, he could shatter the glass with a sneeze.

The purple giant watched Hank leave, then made his way toward the milk. It bent down and sniffed the bowl. We all looked on, hoping to see some sign that it might like our offering. But its face wrinkled, then twitched. Then with no warning, it took in a deep breath and exploded.

Just as I thought! One sneeze took out the entire back door. The door cracked, shattered, and fell to the ground.

Our eyebrows just about jumped off our heads.

"This is so not golden," Hank said under his breath.

Just then, to make matters worse, the doorbell rang. We all exchanged a glance, a "this is not good" glance.

"Are we expecting anyone?" Hector asked.

Still holding our noses, we slipped over to the front window and peered through a crack in the

curtains. Standing on our doorstep was Ellie Einstein, the girl who had started our race on Deadman's Hill. Hank straightened up a little and opened the door.

"Hi, Ellie," he said, smiling the best he could while pinching his nose.

But she did not smile back.

"Hank Hooligan," she started in a not-very-nice voice, "What in the world were you . . ." And that is all she got out before the smell hit her, too. "Uggh! What is that? You guys stink!" she said disgustedly and grabbed her nose. "Do you know that Gwen and I searched for three hours on Deadman's Hill for you and your brothers after that race? No, probably not. Well, we did."

Holding his nose as well, Hank said, "Um. Sorry? I totally forgot after we ran off the road and ended up on Mr. Hudson's doorstep."

"You ran off the road . . . Uggh— that is just gross!"

"You really want to know?" Hank asked. "It's the same reason we didn't finish the race."

"I would like to know why you left us up there, yes. And it better be a darn good reason."

"Not a good idea," Hector whispered.

"Come here and I'll show you." Hank walked Ellie Einstein right through the back door.

When Ellie saw the purple monster her eyebrows squished together. "H-ha-how do you have a huge purple hippopotamus in your backyard?"

"That's why the race was cut short. It jumped out and made us fly off the road," Hank said.

"Why does it *smell* so bad?" She pinched her nose. Then her cell phone rang. She had a little trouble answering it with one hand.

"Yes, Mom, it's me. I sound like a duck because I'm pinching my nose. No, I just ran into something that smells real bad, that's all. What do you need? Yes. No, I *told* him not to do anything with the nano-cell stabilizer! He's probably messed up the whole experiment. Okay, tell him I'm coming."

Ellie turned to Hank. "I gotta go. My gramps needs some help." And with that she turned and ran out the way she came in.

"Ellie! Ellie! Don't tell anyone!" Hank yelled. "Please!"

"Okay, okay!" Hector shouted. "I can't handle the stench anymore." Then he ran into Mom's room. Five seconds later he reappeared with Mom and Dad's laundry basket, and he began hurling all sorts of clothes at the big fella. We watched in amazement as pants, shirts, towels and, of course, socks were swallowed up as fast as he could throw them. All except for my dad's swimming shorts. For some reason, the monster coughed a little when he stuffed those in his mouth—then he promptly spit them back out.

When Hector had nothing left, the monster plopped back on the porch and gave us what looked like kind of a smile and closed his eyes.

"It's asleep," I said. "Talk about bad manners."

"We can't keep this up," Hector yelled. "We're going to end up running around in our underwear!"

"Shhh!" Both Hank and I put a finger to our mouths.

"If it's going to come around every

couple of days and eat us out of all our clothes, by the time school starts we'll be the first kids in history to show up to elementary school in our birthday suits!" Hector continued. At this, Hank did a

double "Shhh!" with two fingers. "Let's not wake it up. We've got to figure out a way to get this thing back up to the hill and keep it there so it stops visiting our house."

"Hey!" I jumped in. "Hank! You're not holding your nose anymore."

"What?" Hector said.

I released my nose, too.

"You're right, little bro!" Hank said. "The smell is gone."

We all took a test sniff and turned to look outside. The giant purple sock eater was still slumped on the porch, snoring.

"It's gotta be because he's asleep!" I said.

"What are you saying?" Hank asked.

"What if he doesn't stink when he's sleeping?" I continued.

"Then it proves your brain is the size of rabbit poop," Hector said. "When we first found it up on Deadman's Hill, it was asleep and it stunk then."

"Well then, prove your brain isn't made of skunk guts and tell us why it doesn't stink anymore?" I shot back.

"It's obviously because he's full," Hector announced.

"Wow," Hank said. "Totally makes sense. When it's hungry it stinks and when it's full it stops stinking."

"Yeah!" I said excitedly. "The other night when it fell through the roof it stunk. But after it ate our underwear I remember the bad smell went away, and then it fell asleep."

"So skunks shoot out stink when they're afraid and giant purple monsters shoot out stink when they're hungry," Hector added. "This thing is weird."

"So then . . . if we can bring clothes up to Deadman's Hill every couple of days, it should just stay up there," Hank pointed out.

But before we could strategize anymore, our doorbell rang again. Maybe Ellie had come back.

We slipped over by the front window and peered through the curtains again.

This time, two pairs of dark sunglasses under two Smokey-the-Bear hats were standing on our front porch.

My eyebrows shot way up.

"We gotta pretend we're not home!" I whispered. "The big fella is right out back!"

But Hank's eyebrows were cocked uneven and his tongue stuck out. He was obviously thinking. Then his tongue slipped back in and he said, "I'm gonna get the door."

"What? Are you crazy?" I blurted back.

"Not a bad idea," Hector said. "Maybe they'll take the big monster with them when they leave."

Hank walked over and opened the door.

"Hello," he said.

The two visitors dropped their chins a little, clearly not expecting an eleven-year-old kid to answer the door.

"Hello, boy. May we speak to your parents?" the woman from two nights ago asked.

"They're busy," Hank said. "Can I help you?"

The woman's mouth crinkled. "This is the Hooligan household, correct?"

"Yes, ma'am, it is," Hank replied.

"My name is Ranger Rabbit and this," she gestured to the other Animal Control ranger, "is Ranger Rocket. We were called in a couple nights back by the sheriff. He reported a very large and strange-looking animal on your street. It was thought to be a grizzly bear. We have yet to apprehend the creature."

"Uh-huh," Hank said. He sounded bored.

"Word from the neighborhood is that your family could help us find that bear," Ranger Rabbit continued.

"Us?" Hank replied. "Really? Well, why would anyone lead you to believe that? We're *awful* at finding bears. Unless you want some gummy bears. . . ."

Hector let out a snort and rolled his eyes.

"I'm not interested in jokes, boy," Ranger Rabbit growled back.

This lady scared me. My eyebrows formed an upside-down V, but Hank didn't seem to be worried.

"Sorry we couldn't be more help," Hank apologized. "But may I ask, ma'am, who told you to come to our house?"

"The tip was given in confidence, boy," Ranger Rabbit said, wrinkling her nose again. "And quite frankly, something stinks about this whole situation. I don't think what you people saw the other night was a bear. I think it's much bigger, and much, much more dangerous."

"BBAHUUUURRRPPPP!"

All of us jumped at the thunderous belch that came rumbling from the back porch.

Hank lost his cool a little and turned to Ranger Rabbit. "Wow, excuse me! I'm really hungry. Hope you find your bear. Thanks for stopping by!" He slammed the door.

"But wait!" Ranger Rabbit's muffled, gurgle-y voice pushed through the door. "What was that sound?"

As I rounded the corner, sure as bees make honey, the purple giant's eyes were open.

CHAPTER 11

One Surprising Stomach

We all just stared at it. And it stared right back.

"What's the plan?" I whispered to Hank.

"No clue, little bro," he said.

The silence was broken by the faint sound of a walkie-talkie and footsteps coming from the side of our house.

"Hank!" I said. "Those ranger people are coming around the house!"

But before I could say anything else, Hank quickly slid the door open and carefully jumped over the broken glass. He grabbed the purple monster by the arm and pulled. But it didn't budge. So I followed Hank's lead and grabbed ahold of the other arm and pulled. Its big eyes looked at both of us, then it ducked its head and took a giant step into our kitchen.

"What are you doing?" Hector blurted out.

We pulled the big fella through the kitchen and around into the living room just as a Smokey-the-Bear hat peeked under the white sheets on the clothesline in the backyard.

"Keep it here," Hank whispered to Hector.

"What? Where are you going?" Hector asked, his eyebrows

pinched together. "There is no way I'm being left alone with this monster again."

"We'll be back in a minute," Hank responded. "Come on, little bro. Follow me."

I followed as Hector continued to whisper-yell at us.

We darted through the hallway and into the bathroom. Hank flipped on the shower and turned on the radio that sat on the counter. Then he pulled my shirt off and wrapped a towel around my head like those guys who charm snakes.

Hank kneeled down by the toilet. "Okay, now climb on my shoulders!" he said.

So I stood on the toilet and threw my legs over his shoulders.

He stood up straight and wrapped another towel around us together, leaving only my head, shoulders, and arms visible.

"Am I supposed to look like Mom in a bath towel?" I asked. "Because her lips are much fuller than mine."

"Just get ready to scream like a girl!" Hank's muffled voice came through the towel. And he wobbled out of the bathroom.

We staggered down the hall

and into the kitchen. Through the broken sliding glass door we made eye contact with Ranger Rocket. I let out the highest blood-curdling scream I could force from my third-grade body. And when my lungs ran out of air, I did it again.

Ranger Rocket jerked backward and stumbled over a planter pot. With his arms flailing, he fell into Mom's rosebush.

A very loud and painful "Ouuch!" came from the fallen ranger. But he quickly pulled himself out of the thorns and grabbed the Smokey-the-Bear hat that had bounced off into the dirt.

I continued to scream. The ranger scrambled out of the flowerbed. Then he hauled buns back around the house. His car keys had slipped half out of his pants pocket and they jingled as he ran, trying to stuff them back in.

I jumped down from Hank's shoulders and hurried to the window. Sure as bugs on a windshield, we watched the Special Animal Containment Vehicle screech off down the street.

Hank barreled over, laughing. "That was GOLDEN!"

I did three rock star fist-pumps, but Hector was not happy.

"The problem isn't over, you cabbage brains," he pointed out. "We've still got Mr. Monster here in our living room!"

Hector was totally right. The big purple fella was sitting on the carpet watching us.

"So, what's the plan?" I asked.

"Did it do anything when Henry screamed?" Hank asked.

"Uh, yeah, the same thing I did—covered its ears!" Hector replied.

"So it can hear us, then," I said. "I wonder if we can talk to it."

"If you can talk to it then tell it to go home. I'll do both your chores and mine," Hector said.

"Well, for that, it's worth a try," I smiled.

"I'll be the one to try," Hank said. He squared his shoulders and raised both hands. "Greetings, big purple friend. What is your name?"

The monster blinked twice at him.

"Seriously?" Hector said, with one eyebrow raised. Then he tightened his lips and let out a high-pitched whistle.

This time, the big fella scrunched his face and reached up to cover his ears, again.

"Well, it doesn't like that," I said.

"At least we got a reaction," Hector shot back, "and not just some eye blinks." Hector lowered his chin and let out the lowest grunting sound he could manage.

This time we got a response.

The big fella lifted its eyebrows and gurgled something back.

"Hey!" Hank said. "That sounds like some communicating to me. Nicely done, bro." Then Hank lowered his chin and grunted too.

At this, the big fella did more than raise its eyebrows. He stood up. Well, as much as it could, its head pressing against the ceiling.

Then it did something none of us expected.

It put a hand on its stomach and opened its belly.

CHAPTER 12

Kapow! Kapow!

All three pairs of our eyebrows shot up and my mouth dropped open. A faint "Holy Hepsibah" slipped from Hector's mouth.

He pulled a book the size of a computer screen from out of his belly, then his belly slapped back shut and he sat the book on the floor. It looked like a normal book except for a little bit of gooey slime on the corner and a latch on the side that kept it closed.

"What's in the book?" I whispered.

But Hank didn't answer. Instead, he took a step toward the big fella and grunted. He grunted back. I could tell it wasn't a mean grunt, more like a friendly, "What's up" grunt.

Hank stepped a little closer. I wasn't sure why he was being cautious now; he'd already grabbed him by the arm and pulled him into the house.

So I stepped up next to Hank and peered over at

the book on our living-room floor. We watched as the big fella opened it up and began flipping through the pages. They weren't paper pages, though. They looked more like plastic, and they had some kind of symbols written all over them.

The big fella kept flipping until he got to one that had a symbol of a seven-pointed star in the upper middle of the page. Under the star there were three large circles and a bunch of squiggly lines.

"Is that Chinese writing?" I whispered to Hank.

"Don't think so, little bro," he said. "Chinese writing looks more like stickmen with hats. This looks like a bunch of squiggly worms with large heads."

The big fella pointed at Hank and then at one of the circles. Hank's eyebrows slanted and his tongue stuck out. The big fella grunted and pointed, again.

"He's trying to tell you something," Hector spouted from behind us.

"I think you're right," Hank said. "But what?"

"Maybe he wants you to sign his little yearbook," Hector said.

Quicker than a jackrabbit, the big fella's hand reached out and grabbed Hank's wrist.

We all jumped back. Hank flinched and tried to pull away, but he was no match for the monster's grip.

"Oh, bag of hair! I told you he's gonna eat us! He's just been playing nice this whole time!" Hector cried.

"Eat a worm," Hank said.

I watched my big brother relax a little. Slowly, the big fella pulled Hank's hand down and maneuvered his index finger onto one of the circles. When his finger touched the plastic page, the circle gave off a split-second flash of light.

"Ooh, that tickles," Hank said. "It felt like eating pop rocks, only on my finger." We Hooligans love pop rocks. We get them at the dollar store.

When the big fella let Hank go, we saw that Hank's fingerprint had been left behind in the circle. Then the big fella pointed

at me. Feeling a little scared, I placed my finger on the second circle. A tingle shot through my skin.

"Wow! That *does* feel like pop rocks," I said.

Then we turned and look at Hector.

"You're up, bro," Hank said.

Hector shook his head. "I'm not in the mood for pop rocks on my finger," Hector said. "What if this giant is stealing our finger-prints so he can make robotic clones of us? And use them to take over the world or something, huh?"

"If that was his plan, he would have just hugged all of us and carried us off," I said.

The big fella opened his mouth and said something, but it sounded more like the big furry guy on Star Wars than words.

"Come on, bro—let's not find out what he's like angry," Hank added.

"Fine, but if this turns out bad, both of you will give me all your hash browns next time Mom makes them for breakfast. Agreed?" Hector argued.

"Done," Hank said.

"Agreed," I said. "But if it turns out just fine, you have to eat ten grasshoppers."

"What? No way," Hector shot back.

"Okay, fine. Three," I countered. "Final offer."

"Um . . . No way again!" he mumbled and stepped up to the book. The third circle flashed and Hector's fingerprint appeared next to mine and Hank's. Suddenly, the seven-pointed star lit up and a symbol of a bicycle appeared inside the star.

"Wow! What's up with the bike?" I asked.

"Maybe he wants a bike for Christmas," Hank said.

"Or it's a sign it's going to steal *our* bikes," Hector added.

The big fella interrupted us and pointed to the image. Then he opened his mouth and tried to tell us something with his mumbling words.

"If he wants to see a bike so bad, let's show him a bike," Hank said.

"What if it eats the bike?" Hector asked. Then he pointed to me. "We're showing it your bike first, Henry. Yours is from a garage sale."

"Your bike *owes* my bike!" I said. "It carried your bike back from Deadman's Hill when you were all wet-noodle-y."

"Eat a worm, you two," Hank interrupted. "I'll show him my bike, since it's the coolest. Maybe he won't be able to swallow it."

We cautiously led the giant out the back and to the shed, where our bikes and our injured Hooligan Hasher were being held captive. Dad had put a large padlock on the door to prevent intruders—namely us—from taking our impounded bikes. But Hank was slick. He pulled a Swiss army knife out of his pocket and picked the lock like a pro. Last summer he'd practiced a hundred times on a lock we got from the dollar store. Hector could pick some locks too, but I still couldn't make it work consistently.

Hank rolled out his bike and flipped the kickstand down in front of the big fella. We watched as its antennae started vibrating.

"And this here is The Beast," Hank said, pointing with pride to his blue and green bike with white wheels. "Well, last year's version."

"What's the plan?" I whispered.

"No clue, little bro," Hank said. "Maybe he just wants to look at it."

Unfortunately, Hank was wrong. It put one hand on each handlebar, swung one leg over the seat, and sat down. The bike was no match for the large purple body.

KAPOW! KAPOW!

Both tires blew and the rims flattened.

"Bag of hair!" Hector yelled. "It destroys everything it touches—even things it sneezes on."

Hank looked discouraged, but he didn't seem mad. "I think he wants to ride a bike," Hank said.

"There's no bike big enough for that," I pointed out. "He'd crush even Dad's bike."

"We just have to find one with really big tires," Hank said. "Or better yet, *build* a bike with really big tires."

Hector's eyebrows scrunched together. "We're building this thing a bike now?"

"Yep," Hank said, "Unless you'd like to let him try to ride yours?"

Hector's eyebrows scrunched even more. "If that thing touches my bike! I'll, I'll . . ."

"You'll what?" I asked.

"Not share any more of my socks with it!" Hector blurted.

Hank and I both smiled. "Yeah, right."

CHAPTER 13

A Field of Stars

We decided to hide the big fella in the shed. It seemed like the logical thing to do. The shed was large—more a second garage really—and we hardly had any other option. It wasn't like we could just walk him down the street. But getting him in the shed proved to be a bit difficult. First we tried pointing and grunting, but the big fella just stood there with Hank's flat-tired bike. Then Hank and I grabbed his arms and led him inside.

"See, Hector, he wouldn't hurt a fly," I said.

"ALRIGHT, BIG GUY, HAVE A SEAT," Hank said. But he didn't move. So Hank and I sat on the ground and gestured for him to do the same.

"Run and grab whatever garage towels are left," Hank said to Hector. "I have no idea how long he'll be in there. And we can't have him sneezing on the house anymore when he gets hungry."

Hector stomped off and returned with a few rags. By this time the big fella had followed our lead and sat himself down, cross-legged. We sat the towels next to the giant and then slowly tried to shut the door. But before we could, a large purple hand shot out and pounded it back open, knocking Hank over in the process.

"That wasn't very golden," Hank said from the ground. "I guess we'll leave it open."

"Then what's the purpose of hiding it in the shed?" Hector asked.

"It's hot out," I said. "At least he won't get a sunburn."

"Your brain has been sunburned," Hector said. "We should just turn this thing in!"

Just then we heard the Big Banana pull up in the driveway. My football watch beeped. It was noon.

"Mom's going to freak out," I said.

And she did.

She freaked out when she saw that the

back door had been reduced to small bits of glass. She freaked out a little more when we told her we'd fed the laundry basket full of clean clothes to the big fella. And she especially freaked out when she caught a glimpse of a purple foot in our shed.

"What happened to my rosebush?" she added with a whimper.

"Oh, that wasn't the big fella," I said enthusiastically. "That was us."

Before Mom could explode again, Hank explained everything that went on while they were gone. Dad's new eyebrow stubble shifted sideways a little when he learned someone on our street had told Ranger Rabbit to come see us.

But Mom didn't flinch. She just knelt down and started picking up the petals that had fallen from her smashed rosebush. I felt sort of bad, like all this was a bit of our fault.

Then Mom picked something out of the rose petals that definitely didn't grow on a flower. "Where'd this come from?" she said curiously.

The rest of us gathered around as she held up a thick shiny coin.

"Is this one of yours, boys?" Mom said.

All three of us leaned in for a closer look. Clonk! Hector's head hit mine.

"Bag of hair!" said Hector, rubbing his forehead. "And you

wonder why we wouldn't let you steer the Hasher—you can't even steer your own head."

"Zip it." Dad interrupted and took the coin from Mom. He displayed it in his palm. On the one side there was the image of a planet with a ring around it. In the middle of the planet was a shield. Around the outside edge were the words *SCUTUM ET PROTECTIO.*

"What does that say?" Hank asked.

"Not sure." Dad said "The last word looks like 'protect.'" Then he flipped the coin over. The words on the edge of this side were long but in English. *World Investigators, Exploring Near-Earth Reports • Directors of Galactic Security.* And in the middle of was the image of a Smokey-the-Bear hat and sunglasses on a face with a large tongue sticking out.

There was no question where the coin had come from.

"Those ranger people aren't part of any animal containment agency!" I blurted out. "They're like, space people."

"What if they're *from* space?" Hank said. "That's why they wear sunglasses at night?" One of his eyebrows up, the other went down and he put a pinky to his mouth.

Hector's eyebrows scrunched together. His lips moved around like he was chewing on an old wad of gum. Then he started laughing.

"What's so funny?" Hank asked.

Hector laughed some more. He was having trouble catching his breath.

"W-w-wiener dogs!" he finally managed to squeak out.

"What about them? I know they look funny, but now's not the time," Hank said.

"No—look at what that spells," Hector said, pointing at the coin. "W.I.E.N.E.R. D.O.G.S." He collapsed, still laughing.

Hank and Dad started laughing, too.

"Wiener dogs . . . from space!" Hank blurted out. And then everyone was laughing, even Mom a bit.

"Well, whatever they are and wherever they're from," Mom said, "the next time I see one of those hats, the person under it will get an earful from me."

Dad slipped the coin in his pocket and put his arm around Mom. "We can fix the flowers and the house, dear. What we can't seem to fix is this purple monster problem."

"Dad, he's not a monster," I reminded him. "Sure, he just about smothered Hector to death, ate all our clothes, caved in our roof, sneezed on the back door, left a little goo behind in the living room, and crushed Hank's bike. But really, does that mean he's a problem?"

"Yes! With a capital *P*!" Hector said.

"You're a double capital P!" I shot back. "Party Pooper."

"Listen to me, boys," Dad interrupted. "I don't want to turn it in to the authorities either, but this can't keep happening."

"We were able to talk with him," Hank said. "Maybe we can train him to stay up on Deadman's Hill."

"Or he could just live in the shed," I said with a smile. "Look at him now; he's quiet as a kitten in there—is that a purr I hear?"

"We still don't even know what it is," Hector grunted. "You want it to *live* in our backyard?"

"You're right, Hector," Dad said. "We don't know what it is."

"But we know what it's capable of!" Hector continued.

Kapow! Kapow! Two more loud pops rang out from the shed. We raced over and sure as cheese on nachos, Hector's bike was ready for the junkyard.

Without hesitating, I grabbed my bike so it wouldn't become the next victim.

"Bag! Of! *Hair!*" Hector yelled. "That's it! I'm calling the Wiener Dog People this instant. AND NO MORE SOCKS FOR YOU!" He pointed a very straight finger at the big fella.

"Dinner, boys," Mom's voice called out from inside. But instead of following Dad and my brothers inside, I plopped down in front of the shed door.

"I tried," I said, looking up at his round purple face and bobbing antennae. "But I guess you eat too much, smell too bad, and crush things like the Hulk. Can't you give me *something* to work with here?"

For a short minute we just sat and stared at each other. If only I had bionic mind-reading powers—then I could see into the big fella's mind. I wondered if his brain was purple. Eventually, I winked. And he winked back. I wiggled my ears. He wiggled his ears as well.

"Hey, that's pretty golden!" I said.

I wiggled my lips, crossed my eyes, and stuck out my tongue. And he mirrored everything exactly. Then I asked him if he would take his book out again, but I could tell he didn't understand. I leaned back and pretended to pull on my stomach.

And it worked! The big fella opened his belly up, again, but instead of the book like before, he pulled out something else. I leaned forward so I could see it better. It was made of the same material as the book, but instead of opening it, the big fella unfolded the object and laid it on the ground. It was covered in seven-pointed stars like the one in the book. And inside each of the stars were other symbols, similar to the bike that had appeared before. There were patches that didn't contain stars, though. The purple giant pointed to these and said something. But I couldn't understand him.

"Cool stuff," I said out loud instead. And he said something back. I wished I had a bionic translation chip in my brain so I could understand.

I moved in for a closer look at the object on the ground and a lightbulb went on in my head. It was a sash of some sort, like the ladies in the Miss Galaxy show wear. Or . . . like Boy Scouts put their merit badges on!

My watch beeped and it startled me. Six P.M. Mom called everyone for dinner for the second time. I knew I'd go hungry if she had to ask a third time. As I hopped up and headed for the house, the big fella opened his belly again and returned the sash.

"I think we should give the big fella something to eat, too," I said as I stepped inside the house.

"Does it smell?" Dad asked.

"Not really." I said.

"You can treat it to some dress socks when we're done," Mom said. "Now please come set the table."

We had some kind of stir-fry for dinner. Stir-fry was code for when Mom takes all the leftovers in the fridge, dumps them into a big pan, and adds rice. But it wasn't that bad this time. At least I didn't gag.

"If we're going to turn in the big fella tomorrow, can I at least sleep out by the shed tonight?" I asked.

"No way," I was told.

After we'd all helped clean up dinner, I stepped back outside. Instantly, the smell of purple stink set my nose on fire.

"Uh-oh!" I said. "I think we've got a hungry monster on our hands."

Hank was by my side in an instant. We ran out to the shed but found it empty. Nothing purple was inside.

My eyebrows dropped. "I knew we should have invited it to dinner," I said.

Mom, Dad, and Hector joined us outside and we followed the footprints in the lawn. But that only led us to our small backyard cement basketball court.

Then we heard it. A bloodcurdling scream came from over the back fence.

CHAPTER 14

Real Live Alien

Sure as slime on a slug, we turned and saw two bobbing antennae in the Woodhouses' backyard.

"How'd that thing get over the fence?" Hector asked.

As we ran around the shed, we could see that its roof and sid-
ing had been splintered apart. Obviously, something very large had climbed it.

Dad quickly ran to the side
of the house and grabbed
the ladder he had been
using and leaned it
against the fence.
In a flash, he
was up and
over and
into the

"EEEEEYAAAHH!!!

Woodhouses' backyard. The three of us boys climbed the ladder and gazed over the fence. We saw the big fella standing by Mrs. Woodhouse's clothesline with a mouthful of pink polka-dot sheets.

"Hey there, big guy," Dad said as he approached cautiously.

Mrs. Woodhouse peeked out from behind a banister on her deck, both hands covering her nose.

The big fella turned and tried to say something to Dad. He gestured with his arms like he was trying to explain a complex idea, but even if we had known his language, we wouldn't have been able to understand anything due to the wad of sheets he was chewing on.

"Are you alright?" Dad called out to Mrs. Woodhouse.

"Yes, just fine, Herman," she replied. "I just wasn't expecting company for dinner. I thought that thing went away a few nights ago."

"Me too!" Dad replied. "It's come back for a visit, it seems."

The giant swung his tail around happily and grabbed the second polka-dotted sheet off the clothesline and started chomping away.

"I wasn't all that fond of those sheets anyhow," Mrs. Woodhouse called back. "I've had my eye on a new floral pattern for the guest room."

"Hector?" Dad said, not turning to look for him. "Would you please go grab some socks so we can lure our hungry visitor back over the fence?"

Hector rolled his eyes. "Yessir." He ran off and returned with two handfuls of mismatched socks he had gotten earlier from the Thrifty-Nifty. He handed them out and all three of us boys began to wave

them in the air. But the big fella wasn't interested in our bait. He seemed to prefer the sheets.

"What's its problem?" Hector asked. "Don't tell me that just because these are secondhand socks they're less flavorful. They have plenty of flavor! Look!" Hector started chewing on a long, striped dress sock. "Come on! Look how tasty these are!"

But still nothing.

"I bet he's full," Hank said.

I agreed. "He just ate two whole bedsheets and a few pair of Mr. Woodhouse's pants."

"I vote to let it stay there," Hector said. "Mr. and Mrs. Woodhouse are nice people. I'm sure they'll have a wonderful time baking blueberry blouse bread and pink pajama pies."

"You'd look good in pink pajamas," I said with a smirk.

"Enough, boys," Dad said. "Throw me your socks."

We tossed them over, but instead of trying to get them, the purple monster sat down and his eyes drooped.

"He's going to fall asleep," I shouted out to Dad.

"Maybe we can carry him out their front yard and around to our house if he falls asleep," Hank said. "Or, better yet, load him in the truck."

PUURRRRR...

Dad put a hand on his hip and scratched his head. As I watched, something caught my eye in the bushes behind the big fella. A second later, a whiskery face popped out from under a bunch of blue hydrangeas.

It was Marmalade, the Woodhouses' cat.

He pawed a leaf and sniffed the air, then looked directly at the enormous purple thing in the middle of the yard. Without any hesitation, he trotted over and rubbed his head, body, and tail up against the big fella.

But Marmalade's kindness was not welcomed.

The big fella twisted to see the cat. Then his eyes bulged and he jumped right out of his socks. Well, he would have if he'd been wearing socks.

He scrambled to his feet and darted backwards, away from the furry intruder.

"It's afraid of an orange cat," Hector hooted.

All it took was one more step by Marmalade, and the monster hauled his purpleness backward right into the Woodhouses' detached backyard garage—wham!—and slammed through the side door. Marmalade started to trot over, but Dad quickly swooped in and snatched her up.

"Oh no you don't," he said. "That building will not be left standing if we let you in there."

Cautiously, Mrs. Woodhouse walked across the yard and collected her cat.

The three of us boys hopped the fence and ran over to Dad's side.

"This is great!" Hector said. "Are you going to keep it, Mrs. Woodhouse? Your garage is much roomier than our shed. We'll throw in two summers of free lawn mowing if you do!"

"Though I do love purple, young man, I think that would be a little too much of a surprise for Mr. Woodhouse," she responded.

A crashing sound came from inside the garage.

"I'm so sorry, Wendy," Dad said. "We'll get it out of there. The plan is to have it gone tomorrow."

Dad approached the garage door and peered inside. I was right on his heels. And Hank was on my heels. But Hector wasn't on anyone's heels—he was petting Marmalade's neck.

Even though it was light outside, it was difficult to see inside the garage. We could make out the large shape near the center, but couldn't tell what he was doing.

"Would you like me to open the big front doors?" Mrs. Woodhouse asked. "The lightbulbs are out in there."

"I think that's smart," Dad said. "I don't think he's going anywhere."

But Dad was dead wrong. When the doors went up, we all leaped out of the way as an enormous purple mass on two wheels shot out of the garage.

"OH MY NOODLES!" Mrs. Woodhouse cried.

I fell backward into a lilac bush, and Hector hit the pavement.

"Ouch! Now it's trying to run us over!" he spouted.

It certainly seemed like it. The big fella had found a bike, and it hadn't been crushed. I looked up to see a large purple tail scoot right down the driveway and out into the street.

"He's riding a bike!" Hank said in utter amazement, then took off after him.

Mrs. Woodhouse's eyebrows squished together and she reached out a hand to Dad, who was picking himself up off the grass. "Oh, Herman, I'm sorry."

"Don't you apologize one bit, Wendy—that thing just stole your bike," Dad said.

"Oh, that wasn't *my* bike; mine's the one with the flower basket," she said. "That's Wendell's old moped."

"Well, we'll get it back for you," Dad said, running off down the driveway. I followed, but Hector stuck his thumb to his nose and wiggled his fingers at me.

Hank and I ran with Dad down the street after the giant grape, but after just a block it was apparent there was no way we could catch up. All three of us stopped, bent over, and put our hands on our knees, out of breath.

"Where's it going?" I said.

"Home, hopefully." Dad exhaled heavily and stood up. "Wherever that is."

We jogged back to the Woodhouses' and assessed the damage to their garage. Mom stood with an arm around Mrs. Woodhouse and Dad reassured her we'd fix it all up.

"But as for Wendell's moped . . . it might be gone for good," he said, his eyebrows apologetic.

"Oh, I'm not too worried," she said. "That thing hasn't run in years. It's quite old, old enough to have to pedal it to start. This whole day has actually been quite exciting."

Hector's eyebrows went up. "And just think—if you kept it here you could experience events like that every day!"

"Yeah, and Hector will come feed him for you," I said. "And cuddle with him at night."

"I'd feed it all *your* clothes!" Hector spat back. "So you'd be naked for the rest of your life."

"Come on, boys," Dad said. "Let's jump in the Banana and sweep the neighborhood. There's a chance we could find it before it causes any more damage."

We said good-bye and all five of us climbed back over the fence.

Hector stayed with Mom. Dad, Hank, and I checked every street we could think of, but no luck. As we drove by the Gas N' Go, Dad's cell phone rang. I could hear Mom's voice on the other line.

"Herman, I can't see it, but I can smell it," she said.

"We'll be there in two shakes of a skunk's tail," Dad replied, hitting the gas.

Hank and I jumped out of the truck as soon as we pulled into the driveway. And sure as slime on a slug, we found the big fella sitting inside our shed, finishing up a large piece of fabric.

"Wait—is that someone's hammock?" Dad asked Mom.

"Looks like it to me," she replied.

And, leaning up against the wall was Mr. Woodhouse's moped, its tires maybe a little flatter than before.

• • •

A few hours later, everything was somewhat under control. With the big fella tucked away in the shed, Hank and I begged Dad to let us sleep on the lawn outside the shed.

"Alright, alright, fine. It'll be the last time this summer," he said. "But I'll be sleeping out there with you."

URGLURGL...

Hector reluctantly joined us and laid out his sleeping bag as far away from the shed doors as possible. As I zipped up my bag, my watch beeped—ten P.M. I looked up at the thousands of stars in the night sky and heard Dad letting out his first snore.

"I don't think the big fella is from around here," I said as I stretched out on my back.

"You think?" Hector asked sarcastically. "You're about as sharp as a cottonball."

"It's his antennae. Only bugs have that sort of stuff. No animals do," I said. "At least not any I've seen before."

Hank shifted onto his back as well. "He could be from somewhere deep in the ocean or deep in the jungle. Explorers are always finding new creatures we never knew about."

Hector raised his head. "You mean the fact that it hides a book inside its belly isn't a giveaway?" He lifted his arm and pointed at the thousands of sparkling stars. "There is no way that thing came from anywhere else but up there."

My eyebrows shot up. "You mean like **OUTER SPACE**?"

"No, the Woodhouses' pecan tree," Hector said, rolling his eyes. "Of course outer space."

For about a minute we all just stared up at the sky, then Hank said, "You're totally right, bro. It's the only logical explanation. We're hiding a real live alien."

CHAPTER 15

Abduction

A*lien* was the last word I remembered before my eyelids dropped shut. It seemed like I'd only been asleep for two seconds when I jerked awake again. I tried to open my eyes but couldn't. There was a low, noisy hum coming from the sky. And a super-bright light shining directly down on us, so bright I couldn't see anything else.

"Bag of hair!" Hector shouted. "Turn it off! If that's you, Henry, I'll give you a triple swirly!"

I turned my head to see him flip onto his stomach and bury his head in his pillow. Hank sat up and shielded his eyes from the light. I squinted at Dad's sleeping bag. He wasn't in it. My eyebrows shot to the top of my head. He had been abducted—and we were next!

Then I saw Hank's body begin to rise.

"No, Hank!" I shouted and jumped like a worm at his legs. I grabbed them and held on tight. "We've already lost Dad—I can't lose you too!"

But Hank didn't go anywhere.

"I'm good, little bro," Hank said, looking down at me. "I was just standing up."

I didn't let go. I wasn't convinced we were safe. After all, we were stuck in a UFO's tractor beam and Dad was missing.

Without warning, a loud voice boomed from above us. "Stay where you are." It came from the light. "Do not attempt to flee."

As the voice gave its instructions, the light shifted from us to spots around our backyard. It finally rested on the shed. I looked up again and could faintly see the shape of a small dark helicopter.

The sound of the blades got louder as it got closer.

Then I felt a hand grab my shoulder. If I were wearing socks I would have jumped completely out of them.

I looked up to see Dad standing behind me. "You're alive!" I screamed. Mainly because I was so glad he'd not been taken hostage, but also because the sound of the helicopter was now so loud we couldn't hear anything. Dad gave me a thumbs-up.

Hector finally jumped out of his sleeping bag, pointed a finger into the sky, and started to holler. But the only words I could make out were "trying to sleep down here!" Then he grabbed his favorite dinosaur pillow, and hurled it right at the light.

A few seconds later a small cloud of feathers fluttered down like snow.

"What's going on?" I yelled in Dad's ear.

"Not sure," he said back. "Let's get you boys inside."

But before I could turn and look in that direction, a rope dropped from the sky, and sliding down the rope came a dark silhouette of boots and a Smokey-the-Bear hat.

"It's them!" Hank yelled.

The ranger landed right in front of the shed, his back to the open doors. His flashlight turned on and caught Hector smack dab in the face.

"**BAG OF HAIR—AGAIN!**" he shouted.

"Hey, you're on private property!" Dad bellowed, but I don't think the ranger heard him. Instead, he swung his flashlight around directly at the shed, but the doors were closed. The ranger stepped forward and reached for the handle. As he pulled, the shed doors burst open with a huge force that knocked him back across the lawn. He landed on his back with an "Uff!" and lay still, knocked out. His hat fell off and I could see it was Ranger Rocket—the same ranger who'd fallen in Mom's rosebushes.

"How'd they know he was in the shed?" I yelled to Hank

"No clue, little bro. But we gotta get him outta here," he said.

We both ran into the dark shed. Once inside, I could see the big fella's face, lit up by his two antennae; they were glowing.

"Quick, cover him up," Hank said, "and pull that gray tarp over the top."

Then Dad appeared in the doorway, saw what we were doing, and gave us a hand. But the tarp kept falling off.

Hank took off his shirt and dropped it over his own head like Little Red Riding Hood. He looked right at the big fella and said, "Hold the tarp like this!" and then held the tarp out to him.

Just as he'd done when he copied me wiggling my ears, the

big fella copied Hank and pulled the tarp over his head, holding it together under his chin. Dad reached up and tied a huge knot in the tarp so he wouldn't have to hold it.

Hank put his shirt back on and pulled the giant purple arm. "Okay, follow us," he said. But the big fella pulled back.

"Come on, big guy," Dad said. "You're under siege. You need to get out of here."

Reaching sideways, the big fella pulled the moped up under his other arm.

"Alright, whatever, if you need to bring your bike, that works too," Hank said. We all stepped out of the shed together.

"Let's get him into the Big Banana," Dad said.

The helicopter had moved off a little ways and was now circling the neighborhood, the enormous spotlight darting all over the place.

Ranger Rocket stirred a bit and tried to sit up. "Hey, stop!" he yelled weakly. Hector stepped up from behind him and walloped the man in the face with a pillow. He fell back to the ground with a groan.

"I really want you to take this alien away, but even more— that was really rude to wake me up like that!" Hector blurted out.

"Go, go!" Dad said. "Around the side of the house and out to the front. You too, Hector! Come on!"

Surprisingly, the big fella carried the huge motorcycle with pedals easily under his arm.

"Alright, up into the truck!" Dad motioned to the big fella. "And you three buckle up inside."

The helicopter was approaching the far end of the house when Dad started the Big Banana's engine. The helicopter's spotlight inspected one of the large pine trees in the back corner of the yard.

The Big Banana's gears shifted low and we rumbled slowly out of the driveway, lights off.

"We just left Mom there!" Hector said. "She's going to be kidnapped and turned into one of those freaky Ranger people."

"I think you'd look good in one those hats!" I said.

"Here, text your mother," Dad said, throwing his phone into Hank's lap. "Tell her to call Sheriff Sherwood, and that we'll call her when we're safe."

Hank did as he was told.

We made it down our street and turned left. A text from Mom appeared on Dad's phone. "The helicopter just left."

"They're onto us," Hank said.

At the next intersection, Dad hit the gas and took a hard right. The Big Banana leaned heavily due to the large load. The big fella hung on in the back, still clinging to the tarp wrapped over his head.

It didn't take long before we heard the hum of the helicopter blades. Then a beam of white light sliced across the hood of the truck. Dad shifted gears and took a left into an older neighborhood.

The trees along the
street were enormous
and shielded us from
view.

"Where are we
going, Dad?" I asked,
"There's no way we're going
to outrun a helicopter. That's like the kiss of death for robbers
on TV."

"We'd have a better chance if we unloaded you," Hector
teased. "Or better yet, that giant lump in the back."

"Admit it, Hector," I said. "You could have turned him in
back at home. Instead, you and your pillow helped us escape."

Hector's eyebrows dropped low. "Someone had to pay for waking me up like that."

"Um, Dad," Hank said, "you do know that this road ends in a very large dead-end barricade, right?" Looking forward, we saw a huge "ROAD ENDS" sign glowing in the headlights ahead of us—and getting closer every second.

"Hang on, boys. Your old man has a few tricks up his sleeve."

As he said this, the engine let out a high whine and we felt the back of the truck bounce up and down. Our heads all jerked back just in time to see the big fella leaping from the Big Banana. He threw the bike underneath himself and landed directly on top of it. It was the type of move that could easily be plastered on the cover of *Fearless Freak Magazine*.

"Whoa! Whoa! Did you *see* that?" I let out. "What a trick, Dad!"

"That wasn't part of my plan," Dad said.

The big fella began pedaling frantically and somehow pulled up alongside us, still wearing the tarp.

The big fella's BMX trick had taken our attention away from the road—even Dad's—and we hadn't realized that we had reached the end of the road. The big fella on his moped and us in the Big Banana all hit the rounded curb and launched into the air, crashing through the wooden barricade, splintered wood flying in all directions. I looked sideways and saw a large, light-purple tongue flapping in the air. I felt my body lift off the seat a little and Hank let out a "Holy Hepsibaaaaaaah!" Hector started to scream.

When we hit the ground, the truck bounced hard and one side mirror flew right off. We heard a loud crunch underneath the truck.

The big fella landed next to us in a cloud of dirt and grass, then barreled straight through a wall of weeds and tree branches. But I lost sight of him as we swerved to miss a large oak tree.

"That was golden!" I let out. I have the coolest dad ever.

"Didn't have that up the sleeve either," Dad said. "Your mom would kill me if she saw me do that with you three."

Everyone inside seemed to be okay, but my ears were ringing from Hector's screaming.

"EAT A WORM!" Hank yelled.

Dad quickly swerved and avoided another huge oak. We were now off-roading through an uncleared field of trees and grass. I looked back to see where the purple giant was, but I couldn't see him.

Dad swerved again and took a hard left. We popped out of the field and onto an old, rocky road. The wheels spun and flung rocks behind us.

"Where are the rangers?" Hank said.

I spotted the hovering light in the sky. "There!" I pointed. "It's following us."

Dad peeled out. Up ahead was a large tunnel underneath the railroad tracks. The Big Banana

revved even more and we raced inside. Dad hit the brakes and we slid to a stop. In front of us was nothing but blackness.

"That was my trick," Dad said, gasping. "But the idea was to still have the big fella in the back."

We sat in silence for a second before Hector said, "Um, so are we just going to hide in this cave forever?"

"We've gotta go back out there, Dad," I said. "We just left the big fella . . ."

"Wait," Hank said. "Look."

Sure as slime on a slug, an enormous silhouette appeared at the mouth of the tunnel.

"Golden!" Hank laughed. "He's still with us!"

Dad started up the Big Banana again. "Okay—this might work after all."

He shifted into gear and turned on the headlights. "Let's go, boys."

"Hang on. We're going *into* the tunnel?" Hector said, pointing into the darkness. "Who knows what's down there? Isn't one monster enough?"

"That's exactly where we want to go," Dad said. "We're going to see a distant relative who might be able to help us. His name is Dr. Brainstrong."

"And he lives in a tunnel?" Hector put both hands on his face. "What kind of family do I belong to?"

My eyebrows went up. "A golden one!"

CHAPTER 16

Dr. Brainstrong

The tunnel wasn't an endless abyss, but after driving a bit longer, Dad stopped the truck. He got out and walked over to the wall. He opened a small control panel that almost blended in to the wall and pushed a button. We gasped as what had looked like a rock wall slid back like a curtain, uncovering a completely new tunnel. He got back in the Big Banana, turned down the tunnel, then stopped and waited for the big fella to ride his bike into the new tunnel. Dad pushed another button to close the tunnel again. And then down the new tunnel we went. We popped out

near the far side of town. Dad killed the lights as we drove out in case the rangers' helicopter was waiting for us. But there was no sign of it.

Dad turned onto an older street where the houses were bigger and more spread apart. The big fella had followed us the entire way and was still on our heels. At the very end of the street was a wide house that looked like a mix between our house and a castle. A large chimney with three stacks rose out of the front. But the thing that stood out the most was the enormous, weathered water tower directly behind the house.

Dad pulled up in front. "Wait here, boys."

He hopped out and ran up to the front door. He knocked four times before I saw it open slightly.

"Um, am I the only one with goosebumps?" I asked. "Dad's not a spy or part of some secret society, is he?"

"It's probably just some old man who goes to Dad to have his dentures fixed," Hector said. "He has

all sorts of weird patients. Once there was a lady who had a tooth ring."

"Ew! How would she eat crepes?" I asked. We Hooligans love crepes for breakfast, especially with whipped cream, chocolate chips, and strawberries. After a minute or two, Dad climbed back in the truck.

We waited for him to say something, but instead he gave us a wink, put the Big Banana in reverse, and inched up the driveway. The back gate creaked open and Dad backed around to the rear of the house. Hector's eyebrows started to go crooked. "Okay, this is getting a little spooky," he said.

Dad climbed out of the truck and we followed his lead. On the back side of the house, a large garage door began to open slowly. We could hear the faint buzz of the door motors. When the sound stopped, our eyebrows shot up. It was the man from the Gas N' Go!

"*This* is Dr. Brainstrong?" I whispered to Hank. "The guy who sells gas and candy and nachos?"

Two seconds later, a girl in flower pajamas appeared at his side. "Isn't that your girlfriend?" Hector asked Hank.

"She's not my girlfriend," Hank spat back. "She's just a friend who happens to be a girl."

"Hey, Hank," Ellie Einstein said.

"Hey . . . Ellie," Hank replied, with a definite question in his tone.

The man walked out towards us. One of his shoelaces was nearly untied and dragged on the ground and he was wearing a polyester Gas N' Go Mart shirt that barely covered his good-sized belly. What I noticed most was the shiny surface of his one glass eye.

"I sure hope those aren't his pajamas," Hector said from the corner of his mouth.

"If they are, he better watch out," I said. "The big fella loves pajamas, and he's probably getting hungry."

The big fella stood next to the Big Banana, his moped under his arm.

Dr. Brainstrong scratched the side of his nose. "Well, blow me down!" he said under his breath. He put a hand to his forehead so I couldn't see his eyebrows, but I'd bet my britches they weren't sitting still. "You weren't pull-ing my leg, Herman. This *is* far from your standard *Felis catus.*"

"What's a *Felis catus*?" I whispered to Hank.

"No clue, little bro," he said. "Maybe he already knows what the big guy is."

Hector piped in. "It's a fancy word for ordinary house cat."

"He said two words," I corrected. Hector stuck his tongue out at me.

Hank spoke up. "Actually sir, he's afraid of cats. Well, at least orange ones."

"Is that so?" Dr. Brainstrong asked. He then circled the giant slowly. The big fella followed him with his eyes and his antennae bent down toward him. The two were definitely sizing each other up. I heard Dr. Brainstrong say a few quiet words like **FASCI-NATING** and **REMARKABLE** and **PHENOMENAL**.

But his inspection was interrupted by the rumble of helicopter blades.

"Ah," Dr. Brainstrong said. "Your assailants haven't given up after all, have they? Hurry, let's get everyone inside."

"Come on, big fella. We're gonna take you inside. You can bring your bike if you want," Hank said. The big fella opened his mouth and said something. I had no clue what it was, though. Hank came over, reached out, and pulled on one of his arms and then he followed.

"I'm still nervous how close you two are to it," Dad said as he started up the truck. The Big Banana pulled through the garage doors just as the light in the sky swept across Dr. Brainstrong's roof.

"That was close!" I said.

Once inside, Hank turned to Ellie. "Um, what are *you* doing here?"

"Me?" she replied. "That's my grandpa," pointing to the Gas N' Go man.

"Your *grandpa*?"

"Yeah, we have the same nose—can't you see it?"

Hank's eyebrows shifted sideways. "Uh . . . sure."

"I come and stay with him sometimes," she said. "We like to make homemade pizza together."

"Do you put pineapple on it?" Hank asked.

"Sometimes."

"I love pineapple on my pizza," Hank added.

But my attention was diverted from their pizza talk to the garage we were standing in. Clearly, this man did not sit and do crossword puzzles in his free time. The room was not small. In fact, ten pickup trucks could have probably fit inside. One half of the room had stacks of random items: car parts, fishing poles, window frames, cooking pans, a refrigerator, sheet metal of all kinds, and, surprisingly, boxes of kids' toys. The other half of the room looked just like what I'd always pictured a mad scientist's lab to look like. Numerous tables were covered in mechanical devices and wires hung down from the ceiling. Beakers and flasks of all shapes and sizes were connected in many different combinations, most with different colored liquids in them. The high walls were lined with hundreds of books that sat on sagging, worn-out shelves. In one corner, a gigantic ray gun stood on a base with wheels that looked like it could be rolled around the room.

And at the center of the room sat a scorched pedestal with what looked like a meteorite resting on top.

For the first time in over a week, I saw a smile appear on Hector's face as he took it all in. "What *is* this place?" he asked.

"Well, young man, this is one of my labs in which I do rudimentary testing of my hypothesis . . . er, hypotheses-es. Drat. I never know how many *-eses* to add to that," Dr. Brainstrong replied. "I just add enough to cover it."

"What kind of hypotheses happened to *that* thing?" Hank asked, pointing to the pedestal.

"Oh, that . . . well, that was my unfruitful attempt to change the chemical makeup of a potato."

"I didn't know potatoes wore makeup," I whispered to Hank.

"Me either," he whispered back.

However, before we could ask more about potato makeup, the big fella turned and took a few steps toward the wall. Reaching down, he picked up a metal bike frame. It looked strange though, like someone had put a tricycle together backwards, with two wheels on the front and one on the back. The monster must have thought it was strange too because he sat down and began to look it over. For a few moments we all just watched him.

"Well then, while our friend seems occupied, why don't you tell me how you ended up with such an interesting creature."

I looked up at Dad with a face that said, "Can we trust this old man? He is, after all, the Gas N' Go guy and puts makeup on potatoes." But Dad just gave me a nod.

We proceeded to tell everything, beginning at our race on Deadman's Hill. He listened intently, adding an occasional "remarkable" and "fascinating." His eyebrows really tweaked when we told him about the big fella opening his belly and pulling out the book. I told them about the sash that was in there as well.

After we'd spilled the beans, Dr. Brainstrong said, "Quite fascinating indeed."

"Hold your horses," Hank interrupted. "Ellie already knew about the big fella—she came to our house and saw him."

"Ah, that she did, young man," Dr. Brainstrong said. "In fact, that is one reason she came to visit me tonight. That, and because we enjoy making homemade pizza together."

"You promised you wouldn't tell anyone," Hank said, giving Ellie a sideways look.

"Grandpa Brainstrong is not just 'anyone,'" she replied, her eyebrows raised and eyelids half shut.

"All water under the bridge." Dr. Brainstrong continued, "Let's see if we can unmask this mystery visitor."

"Wait . . . you're going to rip his face off?" I said. "Pretty sure we're not part of a Scooby-Doo cartoon. He's the real deal. A real live alien; I know it."

"Is that so, son? We'll let's see what we can find out from this alien, then."

Dr. Brainstrong disappeared between two tall shelving units full of equipment. We heard some clanking and banging before he appeared again. In his hand he held a circular device with two wires sticking out.

"What's that?" Hector asked.

"A simple electromagnetic pulse generator," he replied.

"What are you going to do with it?" I asked.

"Well, I'd like to test our purple friend's skin. Do you think it would mind if I gave it a little shock?"

Wait! What? My eyebrows formed an upside-down V. "Would *you* mind it if you got a little shock? Are you going to going to shove tubes in his ears and hook him up to a bunch of wires and poke him with long needles and stuff too? Because if that's your plan, we're out of here."

"Amen, little bro," Hank said.

"Negative," Dr. Brainstorm said with a chuckle. "If my theory is right, I promise there will be no probing, prodding, or poking. This won't hurt him a bit."

I looked at my Dad, and he nodded, raising one eyebrow. We cautiously agreed.

Hector and I distracted the big fella with an old car fender while Dr. Brainstrong stuck some small round things to his skin. When he pressed the button, the purple giant flinched a little but he didn't seem to be too bothered. When Dr. Brainstrong was finished, I saw a small piece of purple skin in his hands.

"Would you mind fetching me some water from over there?" he asked Hector.

"Yessir." And he grabbed a beaker and filled it about half full.

Dr. Brainstrong dropped the skin in the water. The skin seeped a thin purple substance that turned the entire beaker of water purple. After stirring it for only a few seconds, Dr. Brainstrong turned the beaker upside-down and the contents fell out and hit the floor.

"Eureka!" he said. "Just as I thought."

Rather than spilling all over the floor like regular water, it was gooey like Jell-O. In fact that was exactly what it looked like. A big blob of Jell-O.

"**So his skin makes Jell-O?**" asked Hank. "That's golden! I love grape Jell-O."

"No, young man, it's not Jell-O. If I'm correct, it's a defense mechanism. Something very similar is found in *Myxiniformes: Myxinidae.*

"Myxi-what now?" I asked.

"More commonly known as the hagfish," Dr. Brainstrong replied. "They release a type of protein that, when mixed with water, creates a slime that their attackers then choke on. It seems that our friend here did nearly the same thing to you," he nodded toward Hector. "When your saliva mixed with its skin, it made your so-called 'Jell-O' and it filled your mouth. Now, there also must be some chemical in there as well that made you drowsy, but we'll have to do a few more tests to find that out."

"So you got hagfished!" I said to Hector with a smile. "Thanks for being the guinea pig."

"Your face looks like a guinea pig," Hector fired back but it was only half-hearted. I could tell he was distracted. Then Hector asked, "What about when it was holding the fireman's hose? It was wet then, but it didn't turn into a massive pile of purple Jell-O."

Dr. Brainstrong put a hand under his chin. "Yes, wonderful

question. It could possibly be linked to something else as well. You said it lets off a foul odor only when it is hungry?"

"That's our hypothesis," Hector said.

"It is possible that its skin is triggered by hunger as well. I'm not sure. We'll have to see," Dr. Brainstrong continued. "Now we know to avoid the skin if we want to stay awake and alert. I'm also interested in communication. You said you could communicate with it, correct?"

"Um, sorta. Kinda. Not really," Hank said.

"He seems to mimic things we do pretty well. That's how we got that tarp on his head," I said.

"It also tried to tell us something when we were in our neighbor's yard," Dad said. "But it sounded more like a kangaroo call than anything else."

"So you think it *wants* to communicate?" Dr. Brainstrong asked.

"I think so."

Dr. Brainstrong walked to the side door and exited the house. As he disappeared, I caught a slight whiff of stink.

"You guys smell that?" I asked.

"Yes, son, I do," Dad said. "We didn't bring anything with us to feed him, did we?"

"I'm not sharing my shirt!" Hector said. "Especially with a girl here."

"Ellie," Dad said, "is there anything here that the purple

guy could eat? That smell will only get worse if we let him get hungry."

"Does he like pizza?" she asked.

"Nope, just clothes," Hank said.

"Clothes? Okay . . ." Ellie looked confused.

"Or dishrags or blankets," Hank continued. "I'm just worried if we don't get something in his belly soon, you might find yourself without your pajamas."

"Here's a painting dropcloth—will that work?" she said, holding up a sheet splattered with paint from across the room.

It did work—the big fella began chomping away instantly.

When Dr. Brainstrong appeared again, he was holding a device that resembled a calculator in one hand and a leash in the other. At the end of the leash was a goat.

"Hey, look, Henry, it's your twin," Hector said.

"Its ears look more like yours than mine," I replied.

The goat would have looked very ordinary except for the baseball hat on its head.

"Two years ago I came up with a prototype that would allow me to train my goat, Gary, to eat the grass but not the flowers and garden," Dr. Brainstrong said. "However, the only message I have received thus far is something similar to 'Yummy. Food. Yummy. Food.' Over and over." His eyebrows rose. "But what did I really expect? All goats do is eat and discharge. I am curious though . . ." Dr. Brainstrong reached down and fiddled with the baseball hat. Then he took a firm hold of the hat and pulled as hard as he could straight up. Gary's hooves left the ground and the goat dangled a foot in the air. Dr. Brainstrong jiggled the hat and Gary at the same time. Finally the hat let go of Gary's head—

pop!—and the goat dropped to the ground, bleating.

"Eureka! I haven't been able to remove that in a while. The suction was extremely tight."

He turned the hat over so the four of us could

get a better look. Underneath, the surface was covered with small, transparent suction cups, almost like squid tentacles. Each suction cup had a wire running into the center of it with an end that glowed.

"Before you is my first attempt to translate brain activity and neurotransmitter concentration into readable text. The glowing ends of the wires hold electrodes that monitor different regions of the brain. The mental message is then relayed and decoded on this handheld device." He held up the rectangular gadget.

"That was my idea!" Ellie said.

"You mean you can actually *read* the mind of who—or what—ever wears that hat?" Dad asked.

"I remember reading about a mind-reading kit you could buy in *Whacked Warrior Magazine*," Hector said. "But it was gigantic, with spikes poking out everywhere. This is genius! It's perfectly hidden in plain sight."

I tried not to imagine what my life would be like if Hector got his hands on that mind-reading hat.

"In truth, my original intention wasn't to make it out of a baseball hat," said Dr. Brainstrong. "Gary just happens to have a fixation on Hunk Skunks baseball and this hat was the only item he didn't rip off and eat."

"Right on," Hank said. "The Hunk Skunks are on fire this season."

"So you want to try this thing on the big fella?" I asked, uneasy about the direction this might take. The worst-case scenario flashed through my mind. First, Dr. Brainstrong would use a mind-reader on him. Then he'd lock down the purple giant and zap him with that huge ray gun in the corner, and he'd look like that potato without its makeup.

"Correct," Dr. Brainstrong said.

Right then I asked Dad if we could have a Hooligan Huddle.

"Sure thing," he replied. "Dr. Brainstrong, you'll have to excuse us for a moment."

Hector rolled his eyes but locked arms with the rest of us.

"This guy is making me nervous," I said.

"He's a genius," Hector argued. "He knew almost right away why my mouth filled with skin, or slime, or whatever you want to call it."

"Dr. Brainstrong does seem pretty cool," Hank added. "But maybe a little crazy, too. Who tries to talk to a goat?"

"Who is this guy, Dad?" I asked.

"I'll fill you boys in later, but I trust him completely. I think we should give this a shot."

Awesome father that he was, I trusted my dad, and if he trusted the weirdo Gas N' Go glass-eye guy, then I would, too. So we broke the huddle.

"That's quite the impressive way to deliberate," Dr. Brainstrong said. "Are we a go?"

"Yes," Dad said. "But how do you propose we get the hat on its head? Will it hurt it?"

"I have some concentrated sleep serum. If we inject it near an artery, it should work quickly," Dr. Brainstrong said.

"Whoa!" I said. "You said no poking!"

"Ah, yes— that I did," Dr. Brainstrong said. "Well then . . ."

"We just need it to fall asleep," Hector said.

Dr. Brainstrong threw his arms up. "Eureka! Why didn't

I think of that?" He lowered his chin and winked at Hector with his glass eye. "You're a bright bulb, comrade."

Hector smiled with pride.

Dr. Brainstrong donated an old wool suit to the cause. And sure as slime on a slug, within ten minutes the big fella was snoring.

CHAPTER 17

Hoolie Speaks

Even though the big fella was asleep, Dr. Brainstrong approached him cautiously from behind. He held the baseball hat between his two hands as if he was about to put a crown on a king. Both his real and his glass eye were concentrating intently.

"Let's hope he likes Hunk Skunks

baseball as much as the goat did," Hank said. "But how can he not? They've hit more home runs than any other team this year."

Dr. Brainstrong gently placed the hat on the big fella's head. Then, with the palm of his hand, he pushed down with more force. My eyebrows squeezed together. The old man was no longer being gentle.

"I hope he doesn't break that thing," Hector said.

After one last push, Dr. Brainstrong backed away. "I believe we've done it," he said.

We all gathered around Hector, who was charged with holding the decoder. The small screen lit up and a black cursor began blinking on the left side.

"We should be getting some readings any moment," Dr. Brainstrong said, but the cursor just blinked at us.

After a minute of staring at the screen, we all stepped back. Even though we knew it was a long shot, we'd had our hopes up. Dad scratched his head. I checked my football watch. It was four forty-nine A.M.

"Well, it was worth a shot," Dad said with a sigh.

"Perplexing," Dr. Brainstrong said. He placed his hand under his chin and closed his eyes to think.

"If it's not going to work, should we take it off?" asked Hank. "Maybe Gary will want his hat back. The Skunks have a game tonight."

"Does it have an on/off switch?" Hector asked.

"Eureka! I knew I was forgetting something quite elementary," Dr. Brainstrong said. "Just like I always forget my toothbrush when I go on vacation." He marched over and twisted the small button on the top of the hat.

At that instant two things jumped: the cursor on the decoder and the purple giant.

From out of a dead sleep, the big fella's eyes snapped open and took us all in.

"Hey, I'm getting something here," Hector blurted out.

I swung my eyes from the big fella for a split second to glance at the decoder screen. The cursor was skipping across the screen, leaving all sorts of squiggly lines and symbols.

I looked back up. All the pushing Dr. Brainstrong had done to get the hat on hadn't fazed him a bit, but with the turn of a small button, we had a very alert alien in front of us.

The big fella reached up and felt the hat on his head. When he couldn't easily pull it off, his eyebrows dropped. He looked like he was getting angry.

Hank stepped forward. "Hey, big guy. Don't take the hat off. You're lucky! The Hunk Skunks hats are all sold out because

they're the hottest team in baseball right now." The big fella opened his mouth and mumbled something back.

"Step back, son," Dad said. "You don't know what it's going to do."

Hank stopped. And the big fella mumbled again.

"Is that thing working?" Hank asked over his shoulder. "What did he just say?"

"All I see are squiggly lines, like worms with big heads," Hector said.

"The dial on the left, turn that like a radio tuner," Dr. Brainstrong instructed, with some urgency in his voice. "The frequency of its brain is different than a goat's, I'm sure."

Hector did as he was told. I looked at the screen again. The symbols changed from worms with big heads to square shapes with gaps in them. Finally, I recognize a few letters as they skipped across the screen. An *A* ran across, and then a backwards *R* and *T* followed by some other symbols.

The whole time we were trying to figure out the translator, the big fella sat there twitching every few seconds.

"That's the Russian alphabet," Dr. Brainstrong said. "Keep going. Just a little more . . . more . . . Eureka!"

When he said that, I looked down again and found three words on the screen.

"Hoolie brain toot."

"It worked, it worked!" Hector shouted. "There are words! Real American words!"

I jumped in excitement as well. When I settled down, my eyebrows shifted up. "What is a Hoolie? And is that *toot* like '*toot-toot goes the tugboat*' or the *other* toot?"

"Oooh gross," Ellie said.

"Little bro. I have brain toots in science class all the time," Hank said. "My mind goes completely blank and the words Ms. Sara says turn into 'blah-blah-blee-blah-blah.' It's like a mind meltdown."

I looked up and saw the big fella twitching even more now. His belly started to jiggle slightly as well. "I think we're hurting him. He's having a mind meltdown," I said. "What if we're killing his brain?"

The message ran across the decoder again, but now a fourth word had been added.

"Hoolie brain toot tickle."

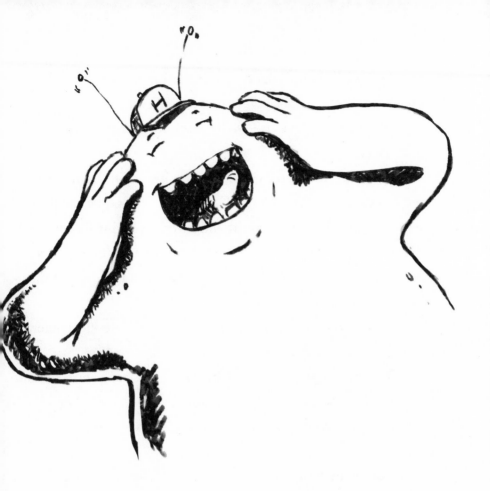

"What in Holy Hepsibah's name is a toot tickle?" Hector asked.

The shaking increased until he opened his mouth wide and let out a loud bellow.

"He's laughing!" Hank said. "I don't think we're killing his brain. We're tickling him, or more accurately, 'toot tickling' his brain!"

The big fella put his hands on his head and continued to bellow with laughter. The laughter was contagious. I started laughing and so did everyone else. Well, except for Gary. He was kind of a serious goat.

"The transmission pulse must be too high," Dr. Brainstrong said to Hector, still chuckling. "Goats have thick skulls and little neuroactivity, so if our purple friend here is at all intelligent, we might be overloading the electric stimulation in its mind. There is another dial on the back side of the transmitter. Turn it to the right."

Hector turned the dial. But instead of a decrease in laughter, the big fella laughed harder.

"Whoops! Maybe it's to the left," Dr. Brainstrong corrected.

That did the trick. As Hector turned the dial, the big fella began to settle down. By that time, a few tears had seeped from my eyes.

Another message appeared on the decoder. "HOOLiE TUMMY TiRED."

"Its tummy is tired," Hector announced to us.

"Mine too!" Dad and I said at the same time. "Tired of laughing," Dad added.

"Now it's thirsty," Hector said, showing us the message.

Dr. Brainstrong walked over and opened an old refrigerator that sat against the nearest wall. "Shall we see if our friend likes orange juice?" All of our eyebrows shot up as we looked over and saw that the entire thing was full of cartons of glorious golden orange juice.

"Well, if he doesn't, I'll take some," I said. Even though it had come out my nose during our race, I still loved the stuff.

Dr. Brainstrong opened the top of one carton and handed it to the big fella. His antennae bent down as if they were inspecting the contents. Then, in one big gulp, the big fella drank it all!

I looked down at the decoder. "Delicious!" blinked on the screen. Then: "Hoolie want more!"

Hector looked at the screen for a moment then said, "I think Hoolie isn't a thing. I think that's its name."

Dr. Brainstrong opened two more cartons of orange juice and passed them over.

"Delicious! Delicious!" blinked again on the decoder.

"He has a name?" Hank asked as one eyebrow popped up. "Good, because I'm tired of hearing Henry call him 'big fella.' No offense, little bro. It just sounds a little funny." Then Hank gave the name a try. "Hoolie. Hooooolie. Hoolie the Hippophant. It's not bad. I wonder how long it can Hoolie-Hoop?"

"Good one," Dad said with a chuckle.

After six cartons of orange juice, the big fell—I mean . . . *Hoolie* wiped an arm across his mouth.

The decoder lit up with the words, "Aaah. Hoolie all done."

• • •

For the next four and a half hours we learned a lot about Hoolie. At one point he opened up his belly—which I still hadn't gotten used to, it just looked so weird—and pulled out his book and sash. He turned to the page where Hank, Hector, and I had left our fingerprints. The seven-pointed star still had an image of a bike in the middle.

"Aha!" Dad said. "You sure did earn that badge, didn't you?"

Hoolie put on his sash. On the decoder, the words "Hector put badge" blinked across.

"Me? Why me?" Hector said. "Henry would clean out your toe jam if you asked him to; have him put your silly little bike-riding merit badge on you."

"Hector put badge" flashed again.

"Fine, fine," Hector finally said, throwing his hands up in the air. "I'll give you your badge. Though your bike is really an old man's moped. But we'll call it good." Hector unlocked the badge with another fingerprint. "Just like pop rocks on my finger," he mumbled. Then he reached up and placed it with the other badges on Hoolie's sash. A giant purple smile spread across the big fella's face.

A second later, my football watch beeped and I looked down. It read 10 A.M. on the dot. I let out a giant yawn. Almost being abducted and barely escaping evil villains in the middle of the night can really drain your energy. Hank yawned too. Then Hector and Dad followed.

"We should get you boys home and get some sleep," Dad said. "Plus your mom has been texting me nonstop."

"I'm just fine," Hector said, stifling a yawn. "I want to know more about those over there," pointing to two half-built robots leaning in a corner.

"Never mind some rusty robots," I said. "I don't think it's safe for Hoolie back home yet."

"We'll have to take him back to Deadman's Hill," Dad said. "That's probably the best place for him."

"If I may interject," Dr. Brainstrong said, clearing his throat, "our purple friend is welcome to take refuge under *our* roof. This lab accommodates his size and I have quite the collection of aging wool suits that I'm sure he'll find extremely delicious." He gestured toward Hoolie. "In fact, it seems . . . oh dear. I wouldn't have thought *that* lab coat would have any wool in it. One of my favorites."

Ellie's eyebrows drooped and she tugged on Dr. Brainstrong's arm. She whispered something in his ear and he whispered back, "Don't you worry about that. I've got everything under control."

"Are you sure, Bart?" Dad said. "That's a generous offer . . . and I don't want to be the reason your wardrobe goes missing. I don't even know how long he'd have to stay. And since you don't carry a cell phone, it might be a little difficult to keep in contact."

"I've got mine," Ellie said. "We can call you. I'll give you my number, Hank."

"Um. Okay," Hank said, and grabbed a pen from a table and wrote it down on the back of his hand.

"We shall take it one step at a time. But you all need some sleep," Dr. Brainstrong said.

"What do you think, boys?" Dad asked, looking at us.

"Sounds like a perfect solution," Hector said.

I looked at Hoolie, who had finished off the lab coat and was looking about as sleepy as the rest of us felt.

"He'll be okay, right? And we'll come back to take him to Deadman's Hill? Tonight?"

"We'll have to see about when we can get him back to Deadman's Hill. But it's a good plan for now, Henry," Dad said.

I gave in and climbed up into the truck with my brothers. Hank gave a peace sign to Ellie and Dr. Brainstrong as we pulled out. We weren't half a football field down the road when my lights went out.

• • •

Dad must have carried us in the house because the next thing I knew, I was awake on the family room floor next to Hector, who was making wounded warthog noises. I poked him in the nose. Nothing changed. Then I licked my finger and stuck it in his ear. One of his eyes popped open.

"Uggghh," he said, putting a hand to his ear. "Did you just give me a wet willy?"

"What?" I said back. "Your snoring woke me up."

He licked his finger and reached in my direction, but I jumped up and out of reach.

"I'm going to stick a tadpole up your nose when I get up," Hector threatened, then turned back over and started fake snoring. His fake snoring was almost as bad as the real thing.

I looked out the window. It was dark. My football watch read 9:38 P.M. I walked into the kitchen.

"Where's Mom? I'm hungry."

"You know where the peanut butter is, Henry. Your mom's still over at the dollar store, I think. Hoolie just about cleaned us out of socks."

Dad's cell phone rang. He picked it up and put it to his ear. "Hello? Oh yeah, Bart? No. A what? *Spaceship?* On the decoder? As in he doesn't *have* a spaceship . . . or he needs *his* spaceship? Wait, what did you say? I can't hear . . . He's *gone?* Just now? Where'd he go?"

Both Hector and Hank walked into the room. "Did I hear something about a spaceship?" Hank almost shouted. "Golden!"

"We'll meet you there," Dad continued. "We can be there in ten minutes. Ten-four. Over and out."

Hector let out a low grumble. "Bag. Of. Hair."

"*Yes!*" Hank said with a giant fist pump. "Looks like our adventure's gone into extra innings!"

"Into the Big Banana, boys," Dad said. "We're headed to Deadman's Hill."

Epilogue

A large, thick finger clicked the button on the walkie-talkie. "Come in, Ranger Rabbit."

"Rabbit here; go ahead."

"Somehow they've disappeared."

"Disappeared? *Disappeared?* That is completely unacceptable, Ranger Rocket," the woman's gurgle-y voice said.

"We lost them near the east side of the town. They entered a tunnel, but never came out. We sent in a search party, but they came up empty."

"Yellow pickup trucks don't just disappear into thin air."

"Yes, I know, ma'am."

"So—they went *some*where!"

"Yes, ma'am. We'll find them, ma'am."

"Negative. Return to base—we have a new lead. A young Mr. Rubinstein has agreed to help our cause and pointed us in the direction of Deadman's Hill."

Brandon Dorman is the illustrator of the *New York Times* bestselling Fablehaven series written by Brandon Mull. He and his wife, Emily, have three sons and one daughter, Ellie, who was born just as he began working on *The Alien That Ate My Socks*.

Some of the Hooligans' escapades and quirks come from Brandon's childhood. He loves hash browns, his grandfather had a big yellow truck that he would ride in on his small farm, and he accidentally knocked his brother's teeth out with a baseball bat. He also likes to dip his toast in orange juice (gross!).

Brandon's work has appeared in children's books and on numerous covers, including the series for Pingo, The Candy Shop War, Janitors, and Mysteries of Cove. *The Alien That Ate My Socks* is Brandon's debut as an author.

Visit Brandon at www.brandondorman.com.